The Seventh Swar

Natasha Sharma is the winner of the inaugural Asian Prize for Short Stories (2024) for her hauntingly lyrical piece, 'The White Noise of Lullaby'. Her debut novel, *Beneath Divided Skies* (2024), was selected for the prestigious MAMI Word-to-Screen Market 2024, won Best Historical Fiction at the Authoropod Literary Awards and was longlisted for the Wise Owl Literary Awards.

By day, she helms an IT firm; by night, she writes fiction and essays that have appeared on platforms like Moneycontrol, Youth Ki Awaaz, and eShe. Nine of her short stories have been featured in international anthologies. She also co-runs BookItUp, a popular author-led club where she interviews writers and champions literary voices.

The Seventh Swar

A Satyadarshi Mystery

Natasha Sharma

PAN

First published 2026 by Pan
an imprint of Pan Macmillan Publishing India Private Limited
707 Kailash Building
26 K. G. Marg, New Delhi 110001
www.panmacmillan.co.in

Pan Macmillan, The Smithson, 6 Briset Street, Farringdon, London EC1M 5NR
Associated companies throughout the world
www.panmacmillan.com

ISBN 978-93-6113-122-6

1 3 5 7 9 8 6 4 2

Typeset in Arno Pro by R. Ajith Kumar, New Delhi
Printed and bound in India by Thomson Press India Ltd.

FSC www.fsc.org
MIX
Paper | Supporting responsible forestry
FSC® C010615

To those who solved the mystery while reheating leftovers and scrubbing sticker glue off old jars.

To the dogs – for the joy, the zoomies and the sniffs of approval.

To chai – for keeping brains awake and the bears civil.

To the mysteries that remain unsolved and still manage to enchant us.

And to the best detectives among us – who know that even when you've cracked the case, if Mama says 'Put on a sweater', you put on the damn sweater.

Prologue

Then

The sword slipped from King Ashoka's bloody hand.

Its fall made no sound as it pierced the earth. His horse neighed and sidestepped, nostrils flaring at the scent of death. Ashoka wiped a river of blood from his brow, the gash above his left eye blurring his vision and turning everything into a reddish haze.

Through the sickly mist, he saw the battlefield was worse than a butcher's yard. Corpses of Kalinga's warriors – his own soldiers – were strewn like discarded puppets. The groans of the dying saturated the smoky air, a sound heavier than drums, tightening around him like a python's coils.

And there he was – Shatrughan, his chief minister, his friend, lying broken. His torso was skewed unnaturally, his head turned towards his emperor, eyes wide and unblinking, full of accusation.

The samrat's gut twisted and he lowered his gaze, guilt flooding him. Only two nights ago, Shatrughan had urged him to hold off the attack until their spies confirmed the enemy's route through the eastern hills.

'Samrat, knowledge – not swords – win wars,' he had whispered. His voice carried a warning. 'One misplaced assumption and we will lose more than men. We will lose our legacy.'

Ashoka had not listened.

His pride had not permitted it.

Now, Shatrughan's blood and that of countless others, soaked Kalinga's soil. A harvest sown in arrogance.

Shatrughan's death was an irreplaceable loss. He was a scholar of the Vedas, a man with deep insights. War didn't just kill bodies. It murdered ideas. It silenced voices that carried light. If a war like this ever happened again ... Who would protect knowledge then?

Ashoka leapt from his saddle onto the blood-slick earth, grunting with pain. He knelt beside his minister's body, ignoring the stinging cuts on his own hands and knees.

He gripped Shatrughan's broken sword and pressed his forehead against the hilt.

No more.

From Kalinga's ashes, I will create something new. A covert army. Not warriors of blood, but guardians of thought. Silent. Unseen. Eternal. They will be the true heirs of India's legacy. The ones who would guard knowledge when kings fall and kingdoms burn.

Above him, the vultures circled, dropping lower. Ashoka rose, his royal blue tunic stained with Shatrughan's blood and that of others.

The vow burned in his chest, seeping deep into the marrow of his bones. The battlefield faded from his eyes, but its screams would live on.

So would the promise he made, kneeling in the ashes of Kalinga.

I will protect knowledge.

Now

The knife grazed the woman's throat. Like a rosary, beads of blood formed under her chin. The man wielding the weapon pushed the tip further into her skin.

'Four of your friends have sung like the proverbial canary, Laxmi. So why do you resist?'

Realization dawned in the woman's eyes. *That's why they weren't answering my calls.* Her chin jutted out, her eyes blazing. 'I don't know what you are talking about.'

'The "I-don't-know" route is tiresome,' he said, laughing raucously. 'Spill the beans or be spilled like beans.'

'No. Do what you must,' she said.

Laughter accompanied each knife thrust as the woman fell; her mind retreated into music – the only home she had ever known.

Her last coherent thought was a rendition of the legendary raga that Ustad Tansen's son, Bilas, had conceived accidentally and sung at his father's death, Bilaskhani Todi. She thought it was a befitting ode to her friends' deaths and her own. Voices that had once carried light were now extinguished.

Like the secrets the septet had hidden for so many years – coded in ragas, buried in concerts no one remembered – the secret the man wanted to hear would mix with her ashes.

The chorus dissolved into darkness.

1

Satyadarshi tapped the graphite pencil against her crooked front tooth as she studied her mother across the table. Ragini was absorbed in the *Bombay Mirror*'s entertainment supplement, a vertical line etched between her brows.

'As it is, your tooth is off-centre,' Ragini said, eyes still glued to the paper. 'Keep tapping and it will fall in line soon.'

Satyadarshi didn't bother replying. She set her sketch aside – her mother's profile captured with a surprising tenderness – and fidgeted with her cup, adding to the constellation of stains their daily tea ritual had tattooed on the table's surface.

Across from them, a neatly folded *Dainik Bhaskar* sat in front of an empty chair. A silent tribute to Ajoba, Ragini's father and Satyadarshi's favourite person in the world. The same chair in which Ajoba once sat, slurping his ginger tea theatrically. Two months had passed since the cancer had taken him, but their grief lingered – tucked into corners, woven into the very walls.

The living-cum-dining room had been his second sanctuary; the first being the music room they all shared. Multicoloured curtains filtered light like a morning raga, slow, tender and humming with memory. The traffic sounds outside were softened by the old trees lining their street and by the thick, time-worn walls of their 1960s building, *Aalaap*.

Lavender walls bore the weight of family portraits, and a grandfather clock, a relic from another century, stood in the corner – a custodian of time. As a child, Satyadarshi had insisted it be called a 'grandmother clock' in honour of her super-strict Ajji, whose devotion to punctuality could put even the finest dabbawallas of Bombay to shame.

Giving company to the standing timepiece was a glass cabinet, its wooden shelves sagging under the weight of the legacy of awards placed on it – Bhairavi Ajji's gilt-edged Jaipur Gharana plaques, Ajoba's etched singing awards, Ragini's glass trophies and Satyadarshi's police brass medals. They glinted faintly, a silent testament to the family's musical (and other) lineage.

The living-cum-dining room held the mother–daughter duo's richest memories. It was where they often returned, sometimes in silence, sometimes with tea and the day's news.

Ragini was very fond of the Page 3 gossip and often inundated her uninterested daughter with it.

'Darshi! Another actress has been roped into the drug scandal! What's the world coming to these days?' Ragini glowered at the paper, then lowered it, her keen eyes catching Satyadarshi's inattentiveness.

'Hmm,' said Satyadarshi. Her detective agency, her rebellion against the family's musical legacy, was teetering. Client footfall had slowed, and the bills were forming a conga line on her desk. Her untouched millet upma sat cold beside her as she scanned the stack in front of her.

'Can you believe this? Amitabh Bachchan *actually tweeted* to the thief who tried to rob the Vishnu temple in Kerala, "T 5467 - Please don't do it. You are dealing with Lord Vishnu himself"! How crass can people get? Robbing God's house!' Her mother's hands shook with outrage, spilling the tea.

Aai's outrage yanked her back to the present, 'It also houses a treasure. Thieves don't care about religion or God.'

The tremor in her mother's voice softened into silence. 'Baba always said locks were for the conscientious. Oh, I still miss him. I keep expecting him to walk through that door, mumbling to himself.' Satyadarshi leaned across to wipe a tear rolling down Ragini's cheek.

'I know, Aai. I also miss him. And his absence ... is a bitter pill to swallow.'

Ragini patted her daughter's hand, and in a not-at-all subtle attempt to change the subject, said, 'I've got my hands on two tickets to Niladri Kumar's concert this evening at the Rang Sharda. What say?' Her eyebrows wriggled like earthworms after rain.

'Yes! Of course, I'll meet you there! Don't be late, like always.'

'*One* time. I was late one time, Darshi.'

Satyadarshi's face parted in a grin and she winked at her mother. 'Got to run. I'm meeting a new client at Nepean Sea Road. Wish me luck.'

'Good luck, beta. Nepean Sea Road, eh? Must be rich.'

Ragini's wormy eyebrows lost themselves in her widow's peak.

I hope so. The commission itself will take care of the office rent for the next three months. 'Should pay on time.'

Ragini frowned. 'Your Ajji and Ajoba trained you themselves! Not everyone enjoys that kind of privilege, Darshi. But you chose to use your God-given talent for meddling.'

Not the lecture again.

But luck didn't favour Satyadarshi as Ragini continued, 'Several generations of our family have been steeped in music, Darshi. You're such a talented singer, but do you care? No, you eschewed it all for sleuthing.' Her mother's pert nose crinkled in distaste. 'Even my brother, Dhrupad, would sing, however tonelessly, to please Aai and Baba. But you remained adamant, just like your father. Where you get the nosy genes, I don't know!'

'Aai, please. I don't have the time for this now.' Satyadarshi stood up. 'I'm off. Toodles!'

'You never have the time to listen to me … '

An unholy screech pierced the air and assailed their ears. *Saved by the discordant bell.*

The relentless plucking of tanpura strings jarred Ragini. 'I'd better go, my ten-minute break's over, and the students have probably finished their writing,' she sighed. 'Back to teaching the tone-deaf brigade. See you at the Rang Sharda at seven.'

Before she could escape, Ragini rushed back with a yellow-coloured sunscreen tube in hand, like it was holy water.

'Darshi, don't forget to apply this cream on your face and arms! I got a new one for you – SPF 50! Imported, no less.' She leaned in, inspecting her daughter's face like a jeweller evaluating flawed emeralds. 'The last one didn't seem to work. Your freckles are spreading faster than gossip at a satsang!'

Satyadarshi rolled her eyes. 'You say that like it's a crime. Bye now.'

Ragini didn't miss a beat. 'In our family? It *is*. Bye.'

Grabbing the cream, she hurried down the stairs and slid into her trusty, slightly dented Alto-800, nestled under the gulmohar tree, and then nudged it into the snarling sea of traffic. While she navigated from Dadar to Sion, Satyadarshi's hands moved rhythmically over the steering wheel. The Alto's scratchy music system belted out 'Sitargaze' by Niladri Kumar. The sitar's notes drowned out the cacophony of external sounds, relaxing her.

This is what heaven feels like. Angels playing sitar.

An unexpected call from her father interrupted her ruminations. Her parents were separated but not divorced. Satyadarshi and her father had always been close, but the breakdown in her parents' relationship a few years ago erected flimsy walls between them. She knew Aai was distraught, and despite Appa being just as upset, Aai had needed her more. Though she still didn't know why, their marriage had soured. It doesn't matter how old you are; Indian parents never treat you as an adult. Your business is their business, but their business is just their business.

The phone stopped vibrating, and Appa's photograph disappeared from her screen.

Five calls in one week! I should meet him soon. But for now, music.

The current soulful track melted into another piece, 'Beyond Time'. As Niladri Kumar coaxed sounds from his sitar, Satyadarshi's mind followed, leaving behind every stray thought – weightless, sensuous, beyond time.

⌘

Earlier that night, in the heart of Aarey Forest, the rope, doused in alcohol, was like putty in the hands of the fire. The flames devoured the strands, dispersing heat and fire evenly. The glow from the fire cast shadows on his face as he stared at it. As the flames hissed and cracked, his lips moved soundlessly at first, then the incantations became vocal.

They competed with the fire for attention.

His fingers moved rhythmically over the jaap mala beads, chanting while caressing each bead, then repeating the gesture and the mantra. Each repetition of the Maran Mantra carved a path of obliteration.

Om visvaaya naam /

Gandharvalochni naami lousatikarnai /

Tasmai vishwaya swaha ||

Beads of sweat ran from his temples down to his

collarbones. Exhaustion lapped at his consciousness, but he kept chanting, keeping a vigil by the fire.

The night's exertion had pushed him beyond his limits. It wasn't easy thrusting a knife into a human body repeatedly, watching as life drained out, but despite the fatigue, he was pleased with himself. He was one step closer to his end goal.

But then his thoughts flitted to *her*. His lips curled in disgust.

Always intruding in places she didn't belong. So typical of her. I won't let her spoil anything ever again. This will end in my favour. It must.

The mix of chirps, screams, squeals and growls of the Aarey Forest served as the background score to his chants. The forest ghost flower – the *Aeginetia indica L.* – a holoparasitic plant, glowed in the firelight and swayed with the intensity of his movements. It made him feel at home.

Like the flower, he too was a ghost. Rootless, feeding off others for survival. The last remnant of his family.

Drawing his mind back to the incantations, he timed the 108th recitation of the death chant from the Rudrayamala Tantra family to perfection, finishing just as the embers stopped glowing. They had taken their fill.

His fingers flew over the beads. Clack. Clack. Clack.

With his other hand, he pushed the lank hair from his eyes. The purifying fire had destroyed the evidence. His breath came in sharp spurts. The jaap mala slipped from his exhausted grasp, beads rolling and settling near the extinguished fire, covered in ashes.

There could be no mistakes. Not with this.

The rites weren't superstition; they were calibration. He first learnt Tantra Vidya not in an ashram but from a forgotten man – a scholar of dark rites – in a crumbling temple buried beneath moss and time.

Each chant stripped away his doubt, steadied his hands and bound his will to the task ahead. It unlocked what had been guarded for centuries, bringing him closer to his goal: to be the only one who could open the doors and accomplish what others believed impossible. It was *his* alone to claim.

And like the flames before him, he would annihilate anyone who dared to stop him. Their end had already begun.

He picked up the still-smoking ash and smeared it across his forehead and upper body. Mixed with sweat, the ash formed a thick slurry over his skin. Speckles flickered across the dial of his black Titan watch, obscuring time.

His voice came out as a whisper.

Swaha.

2

'My grandmother was eighty, but she was fit as a fiddle. She ran marathons and held her own against twenty-year-olds. I can't believe someone stabbed her. Why?' Hariesh Pancham said, dabbing a moist, monogrammed handkerchief at the corner of his eyes. 'It's such a senseless act.'

He took a deep breath, fighting for composure. 'After Ma died, Nani raised me while running her company, never missing a PTA meeting *and* always hitting her quarterly goals of crores. She was always ready for a hug and the occasional slap too.'

Hariesh stopped to blow his nose, his head resting back on the teal, pure leather sofa. Satyadarshi paused her furious note-taking – Laxmi Pancham, aged 80, stabbed to death – and looked up. Everywhere she looked, elegant opulence screamed its presence throughout the rectangular, plush-carpeted room. French windows lined one side of the room, opening onto the verdant terrace and a greenhouse.

Paintings hung on most walls, and Baccarat crystals adorned every available surface. In the bar behind her, the precariously hanging wine glasses probably cost more than her age-old apartment in the Hindu Colony.

Not really. Every crack in our flat is filled with memories. Every stain has a history. No Baccarat crystal could match that.

'My persistent pressure on the police has had no effect; the case remains frustratingly cold, and they have already relegated it to the back burner. Who cares about an eighty-year-old's death? She was due for it anyway, is their rationale.

'That is the reason I hired your agency. My CFO recommended your services and was impressed by your sensitive handling of her case. And of course, my assistant researched you and your prior connection to the police, along with your stellar reputation there despite your exit, is definitely a feather in your hat.'

She inclined her head in acknowledgment. 'Any potential business enemies, Mr Pancham? Or personal ones?'

'Plenty for me. But Nani no longer played a role in the company, so it just doesn't add up. If anyone wanted to harm me, my immediate family would've been targeted, not her. What's the point of killing an ex-employee? She left the company decades ago, devoting herself to charitable work. That's why her murder makes no sense.'

'What about your father?'

'Papa was an Air Force pilot. I was six when he lost his life during a rescue mission gone wrong. Within a year, I had lost my mother to a brain aneurysm, and my paternal grandparents had passed on before I was born. Nani was all I had left. She meant everything to me ... Everything,' his voice cracked at the last word.

'When and how did you come to know about your grandmother's death?'

'When Nani missed her lunch date with her marathon folks, they were suspicious. She is usually the first on the scene, and when they called her mobile, there was no answer. And it so happened that the last weekend of every month is our staff's holiday. My grandmother's ... the ... event ... ' His composure cracked, a visible shudder running through him. Without a word, Satyadarshi handed him a glass of water and looked away, giving him the dignity to gather himself.

'I'm sorry. I'm still trying to come to terms with what happened to her. My Nani was murdered during that week, while she was alone in our apartment.'

I wonder if the killer knew about the staff holiday?

Hariesh picked up steam. 'My wife, Sunanda, and our kids were in Paris for a fashion show, and I was in Shanghai when Nandini, my assistant, called me about what had happened. The police found her in the bedroom, gagged and hogtied. She was stabbed seven times! Seven!

'I was spared the sight, but the crime scene photographs are enough to haunt me for the rest of my life.'

'Did the police find anything of relevance? And what about the CCTV footage? I spotted one in the lobby downstairs and a few more in your apartment as I came in.'

Hariesh nodded. 'The police said no DNA was left at the site except Nani's and, of course, ours. The killer likely used gloves and bleached everything he touched. They found traces of the chemical in her room and other places. About the CCTV in the lobby, it hasn't been functioning – out of commission for over a month despite my complaints to the chairman. It's sheer apathy from our society. After the incident, they replaced all the cameras, but how does it help me now? Or our case?'

Hariesh took a shaky breath, regret lacing his words. 'The ones in our apartment captured a grainy picture of a figure dressed completely in black with a ski mask over his head. Last month, a rare power surge affected the resolution of the cameras, and this glitch reduced their picture quality. I was going to get it replaced, but … If only I had done it, we could've captured more details of the killer. Probably captured him, too.' His lips curled down. 'Nandini will send over the CCTV recordings to you, however useless they are.'

'May I examine her bedroom where it happened?'

'Of course.' Hariesh patted his chest and withdrew a cheque from his sky-hued pocket of his coat. He handed it to Satyadarshi. 'This is 50 per cent of your fees upfront. There's a bonus if you identify the murderer before the police do. At the rate they're going, you'll earn it in no time. I'll do anything to catch her murderer. That's the least I can do.' Determination glinted in his black, beady eyes.

Satyadarshi pocketed the cheque. *Hello, money. My best friend. And who uses cheques anymore?*

As soon as she could extract her 5 feet 8 inch frame from the clutches of the suspiciously squishy sofa, they moved to a large, airy chamber painted in a soft shade of blue.

'I haven't touched anything since the day of the murder. Once the police wrapped up their forensic examinations, my staff just cleared the residual debris they left behind. Everything else is as it was on that fateful day.' He averted his eyes from the stained carpet. 'I wanted to preserve the scene. I've also seen the CSI shows.'

He looked around the place. 'I want to stay here, but Sunanda and the kids refuse to live in this apartment anymore. I understand why, though. It makes us feel vulnerable – attacked in our own house.'

'Was anything missing from the room? Did the killer take any valuables?' Satyadarshi asked, bringing his attention back to the room.

'No. Besides the upturned chair and blood, he didn't disturb anything. Nani's credit and debit cards, along with cash, were untouched. Not even the jewellery she wore!'

Satyadarshi scanned the space. A wall-to-wall bookshelf dominated much of it, and a ladder-cum-chair was propped against the rack. A peacock-blue easy chair with a matching ottoman completed the cozy picture. Satyadarshi could almost imagine Laxmi seated on it, reading a book with her feet dangling over the ottoman, with a cup of tea by her side.

Heck, I can imagine myself doing that.

Hariesh caught her looking at the volumes. 'Nani found reading very relaxing.'

'A great habit.' Satyadarshi walked up to the shelves and ran her fingers over the leather-bound, mostly first-edition books. Their padded covers felt luxurious to her touch. A tatty cover caught her eye. It looked completely out of place among the glamourous books, and she withdrew it from the rack. She wasn't sure what made her reach for it – instinct, perhaps, or the dissonance of something humble in a room designed to gleam. It was a thin book titled *Origin of Music Across Indian Temples*. Satyadarshi recognized it but couldn't remember where she'd seen it.

Maybe on the bookshelf back home?

'Was your grandmother inclined towards music?'

Hariesh cocked his head. 'Not particularly. I mean, she listened to classical music – Indian and Western – but she didn't play any instrument.'

Satyadarshi nodded as she flipped through the book. It was a few pages thick, with an old-fashioned picture and a few mantras inside. There were scribbles on the margins. The text in this one differed from the one she had at home, as did the illustrations – this version seemed to align with an entirely distinct set of swars, though the title was identical. *Odd*. She replaced it and rubbed her hands briskly.

'Mr Pancham, I need access to her mobile phone records and related documents – her will, bank statements and so on.'

She looked around the vast room. 'I need to search this room thoroughly, just in case I find something important. May I do it now?'

'Sure. I'll leave you to it. I've got to get back to the office, anyway. When you're done, just inform my housekeeper.'

Hariesh nodded at her and exited the room. The door closed softly behind him. A strange silence lingered – like the pause before a note is struck. As a child, she had heard that same silence in concert halls before her performances.

Satyadarshi put on her gloves and got to work. She moved towards the walk-in closet. It was full of sarees and shoes. The drawers and their grooves were all empty – no secret shoeboxes with photographs or other interesting titbits. Marathon medals, hung on a hook behind the door, clinked gently as she shut the wardrobe.

The bathroom was clear too, holding only bottles and medicines. She raised the cistern's ceramic lid, but nothing was taped to it. Disappointed, Satyadarshi moved to the centre of the bedroom.

Blood pooled on the cream carpet, had dried into almost-black patches. The chair cushion was also stained with faint smears. The wall opposite the chair was speckled with blood spatters – some reaching as high as the ceiling.

A writing desk stood sentry in front of wall-length windows overlooking the building's lawn. The blinds were drawn up, and sunlight flooded the room. She walked to the ornate desk and opened the drawers with a little extra force; the sound echoed in the silent place. Sadly, they were full of pens and several sheets of official-looking papers. The indigo leather chair showed evidence of copious blackish patches.

Zilch.

A queen-sized bed sat at a right angle to the desk. The teal blue bedspread also bore the telltale crimson drops. Satyadarshi raised the mattress and looked under the bed; it was spotless. A search of the side tables yielded only chargers and a battered mobile.

Exhaling loudly, Satyadarshi punched her fist into her palm as she scanned the room.

Absolutely nothing. Seven stab wounds seem like a personal attack. Not a professional execution scene, this. Why would the man then kill an old woman with no intention of robbery? And leave the scene with no DNA? Or scrub it all off? I think the answer lies in her life, probably not connected with the company.

The sunny bedroom emanated tranquillity but offered no clues. With slumped shoulders, she moved towards the door. As she stretched her hand to grasp the doorknob, her eyes fell upon a wall hanging.

A blue banner with tassels in red, brown, green, blue and other jewel tones. At its heart, a seven-pointed star framed a golden musical note, flanked by a nightingale and an eagle.

Someone sure liked music.

Her eyes widened as she connected the dots. *Music!*

Satyadarshi jogged to the bookshelf and retrieved the thin book. She flipped through it again and, shaking her head, placed it in her bag, making a mental note to inform Mr Pancham about it.

With a last look around, she padded out of the room.

3

The little bell chimed as Satyadarshi walked into her small-but-sufficient office in Laxmi Baug, Sion. She hummed under her breath. The Pancham residence had yielded nothing remotely clue-shaped, but that didn't kill her good mood.

Today, no idiot had hijacked her parking spot, letting her glide the Alto in like a queen in scuffed loafers. This was why she loved her compact car. It may be battle-weary and had a horn that wheezed like a busted guitar, but damn, it was easy to navigate. *And* park.

Greeting her assistant, Twarita, who was on the phone, she ducked into her inner sanctum. Satyadarshi flung her handbag onto the table and made a beeline for the tiny bathroom, washing her face with the ubtan face wash her mother insisted on.

Apparently, it was great for de-tanning.

She examined her reflection. Sleep had been elusive lately; dark circles framed her hazel eyes – her lineage's unwanted gift, which always attracted unwanted attention in her opinion. The kajal pencil she swore by invariably smudged, turning her into a raccoon with crime-solving credentials. Satyadarshi peered at the spots on her pert nose.

More freckles today. SPF 50 clearly hadn't received the memo.

She grinned and left them be.

I won't let Aai sway me. I like the nose-covering freckles.

She then remembered what her mother had said about them.

'Gossip in a satsang!' Seriously, Aai and her similes. I should start compiling a list of them. Aai's Similes, Vol. I: The Audacity Edition.

Sniffing her armpits, she reapplied the deodorant. The faint scent of Nivea cream and Nilgiri oil followed her. The soft, talcum-powdered scent of Nivea products always reminded her of Ajji, who was a massive fan of the cream and used it copiously.

Those FMCG folks must love the month of May! Maximum sales of antiperspirant products and perfumes. If I could change one thing about Bombay besides its traffic, it would be to reduce the duration of this sultry weather.

Feeling marginally better, she straightened her white muslin tunic, padded out towards the mini refrigerator in the corner and, plucking a masala buttermilk carton out, turned the air-conditioning on. As she sank into her chair, the ergonomic arms squeaked in solidarity.

If this were self-care, Satyadarshi figured she was nailing the detective edition of it.

One thing her Batmobile sorely lacked was an efficient air conditioner. Her car, with its wheezy cooling system, was a mini-oven-on-wheels, losing the daily war with Bombay's humidity. She was the sweaty collateral damage, spoils of the water vapour war.

But now in her cooling office, a small sigh escaped her, and she brought the straw to her lip, taking a long sip. Her thirst slaked, she fished out the book from her bag – *Origin of Music Across Indian Temples.* It didn't look like much. Thin. Tatty. But something about it refused to leave her alone, her instincts whispered it was important, but her brain argued its correlation to the case.

Let's see what's inside.

The notations were scribbled in black ink. Years of reluctantly absorbed musical theory enforced upon her by her grandparents and mother kicked in, and Satyadarshi recognized the reproduced painting as one of the Ragamala. It showed a woman, probably a royal princess or nayika – as Satyadarshi remembered was the actual word – seated on a carpet on a palace veranda, surrounded by blooming lotuses and strutting peacocks. A veena lay next to her, and an expression of longing echoed across her face. Other pages had a few mantras, but the last page caught her interest.

Om Tatpurushay Vidmahe /
Suvarnapakshaya dheemahee /
Tanno Garudah Prachodayat ||

She recognized it instantly as the Garuda Mantra. Her father, in happier times, chanted it every morning. She'd sit on his knee and chant along, fumbling with the words, but earnest. Later, she'd sit by his side, chanting with confidence. That ritual, like so many others, had quietly crumbled.

A smile blossomed on her lips when she remembered the text message he had sent her this morning.

I'm happy that Appa wants to meet me. Maybe we can repair our relationship. And maybe even Aai and Appa can rebuild theirs. Hope springs eternal.

Turning her attention back to the case, her smile melted away.

Clearly, this book is of no use in this case. Wrong number, instincts.

Twarita knocked on the door just as Satyadarshi was aiming to launch her finished carton in the trash can. The box fell right into the centre, spinning before settling down. Twarita burst into applause, grabbing her mobile as a pretend mic to mimic a sports announcer's dramatic commentary.

'And Satyadarshi takes the basket, giving India the much-needed last point to destroy the opponents. This is not only Satyadarshi's victory but the entire country's win! Congratulations to the talented sportswoman!'

The two women giggled.

Twa is a sister from another mother. A less dramatic mother, for sure.

Returning to the business at hand, Twarita took down notes as Satyadarshi recited the facts of the case.

'Maybe the telephone records will reveal some hidden details, SD,' said Twarita, shutting her notebook. She was a firm believer in writing things down on paper.

'From your mouth to God's ears, Twa.'

The tinkling bell indicated a client's arrival, cutting their conversation short. Twarita rose to open the door and returned with a lady in her wake. The client brought with her, a deep floral scent that tickled Satyadarshi's nostrils, and she controlled the urge to sneeze.

A tall woman in a rose-pink Lucknowi saree walked in like she owned the lease to glamour. Her blouse plunged, her bun defied gravity and her salmon-coloured sandals clacked with designer entitlement. She patted a few stray tendrils in place as she made her way to where Satyadarshi sat.

The woman's kohl-lined brown eyes darted around the office as she clung to her designer handbag, her gaze skimming over the certificates on the wall and the trophies lined up on the shelves. Her eyes dwelled on a newspaper cutting of Satyadarshi hugging an old woman in a traditional Navari Kashta saree – Satyadarshi's first case, where she had located the woman's missing daughter and rescued her from traffickers.

She surreptitiously adjusted her palazzo pants and rose to greet the client.

'Hello, I'm Satyadarshi. Welcome to Siddhi Solutions. How may I help you?'

'Hi. My name is Preia. I'm a social media influencer. And I need your help to solve a *grave* problem.' Her voice was cultured, with a hint of the posh South Bombay accent.

'Of course, Preia. Why don't you have a seat? Would you like something to drink? Perhaps, some cool sugarcane juice?'

'Oh, that'd be lovely. The humidity is killing me today.'

Twarita brought in two chilled glasses and offered them

to her boss and Preia, then withdrew from the room, leaving the two alone. Satyadarshi watched as Preia photographed the quickly sweating glass, taking various selfies with it. Satyadarshi hid her smile as she relished the sweet–spicy rush of her ginger-tinged sugarcane juice.

Once Preia was done, she took bird-like sips. 'I'm a mommy to a fur baby – a pug, Baby Bimbette. He's the most precious thing to me. I love him so much, and this is why I need your help.'

'Okay. Can you elaborate?'

Sheesh, what sort of name is that? Baby Bimbette?

'Well, frankly, Baby Bimbette has become obese,' she said, her rose-tipped fingers fluttering in the air. 'He's turned into quite the rotund little dog. I even hired a walker who claims he takes him out for two kilometres every day, but despite all the exercise, my poochie-poo just keeps gaining weight. He is like a ... sausage with eyes, feet and a tail.'

'Well, Preia. I'm not sure how I can help here.'

'I want you to follow Baby Bimbette.' Her eyes homed in on Satyadarshi's.

'Okay. How will my following, err ... help Baby Bimbette?' Twarita's raucous laugh, disguised as a hacking cough, filtered in through the closed door.

'I've got a sneaking suspicion that Baby Bimbette is stealing food from my fridge. I don't know how he manages to open the door, but I'm ready to double your fees if you can tell me how he's getting so roly-poly!' She pointed at herself. 'Have you seen me? Someone as slender as I am, needs to have a poochie-poo who's equally slim. Baby Bimbette is spoiling my image. Pet brands are jumping off my ship like rats.'

Suddenly she banged the glass on the table, startling Satyadarshi. 'I am bleeding money! I just lost a fifteen-lakh deal with a leash company. And the dog is still fat *and* getting fatter. This won't work for me. His waistline is swallowing my deals!'

Satyadarshi nodded in sympathy.

She gets fifteen lakhs to pose with a dog?! And I'm chasing murderers for lunch money. Who made these career charts, and why wasn't I consulted?

Preia's botoxed brow resisted the frown that dared to form as she continued her rant. 'And what am I besides my image? And of course, Baby Bimbette's too. So, will you take the case?'

Satyadarshi pondered over it.

It would be easy money, and I'd get to spend time with a dog. Win-win!

'Sure, Preia. Twarita will handle the paperwork and the payments. Please send us the latest pictures of Baby Bimbette and your dog walker's contact details.'

She watched as Preia strutted out, her sandals clacking against the floor.

No ego when it comes to money.

4

The next morning, rejuvenated by the Niladri Kumar concert at Rang Sharda, she beat Twarita to the office – a rare feat – and rewarded herself with tea from the barely functional kitchenette.

Hariesh's assistant had emailed his grandmother's itemized bills for the last six months, along with other papers and the internal surveillance recording. Satyadarshi switched on her laptop and dove in.

She watched the videos, but she could barely tell if the scuttling figure on the screen was even human. The camera in Laxmi's room had been intentionally shifted, leaving the actual murder outside its frame.

No sound. No screams. No salvation. The CCTV glitch had turned the room into a theatre of silence. And Laxmi's phone – the last witness – was smashed beyond retrieval.

Pushing her laptop aside, she plugged in her earphones and put on her favourite classical music playlist. Sliding on her reading glasses and waving a hello to Twarita, Satyadarshi settled back with another cup of masala tea and a highlighter pen.

The glorious part of being a private detective: digging through phone records.

Three hours and a blaring headache later, she had shortlisted sixteen of Laxmi's regularly corresponded numbers. She eliminated half, verifying them against the list of known numbers Hariesh had provided.

I'll call them one by one, especially the ones she dialled a fortnight before her murder.

Three of the numbers belonged to Laxmi's running mates. Out of the remaining six, five went unanswered. A man named Mr Chopra answered the last number. The phone, he said, had belonged to his father, who'd died of a heart attack a week ago.

A couple of deaths. Related?

Satyadarshi doodled on her pad as she fixed a meeting with Mr Chopra. Her pencil absentmindedly sketched a pug's squashed little face.

Baby Bimbette is clearly living rent-free in my brain.

Staring at the remaining five numbers, she called in favours from her contacts at the mobile companies, begging for details. Within a few minutes, she (illegally) received the information of those subscribers. The numbers belonged to Mr Shadaj, Mr Gandhar, Mr Dhaivat, Mr Raag and Ms Madhyama.

Her gaze flicked to the book on her desk.

Shadaj, Gandhar ... aren't those swars? Coincidence? A pattern? Musical elements persist.

All the phones except Mr Dhaivat's showed almost no

recent activity. She saved the numbers on her phone before examining the will and bank statements. Her mobile's contact list was always a mess – an archaeological site of past and present cases. Once a quarter – if she remembered – she deleted them; otherwise, they stayed put. Unless Twarita intervened, angel that she was!

Putting the papers aside, she rubbed her tired eyes as she leaned back in her chair. Exhaling deeply, she checked her watch and decided it was time to meet Mr Chopra. She texted Twarita the address and trudged out to her Alto.

⌘

Satyadarshi parked her Alto in a lane adjacent to the dairy shop on Worli sea-face. The address led her to a grey marble–covered bungalow with a fleet of expensive cars parked outside. Her tiny Indian-made car looked forlorn and lost among its foreign counterparts.

Rich people keep rich company. Huh, the cost of my Alto is probably less than that of their tyres!

She walked up to the mahogany door and rang the bell. A uniformed maid ushered her into the lobby, where a tall man with greying hair stood. He had stooped shoulders and a burgeoning paunch. Dressed in a dark maroon pinstripe suit, his red tie gleamed against a crisp white shirt. Smiling eyes gazed at her from beneath a bushy unibrow, flowing into a bulbous nose and a strong, clean-shaven chin. A spicy musk aroma surrounded him like a cloud.

'Hello, I'm Naad Rishabh Chopra.' He held out his hand – soft and pudgy.

'I'm Satyadarshi.'

Satyadarshi was immediately enamoured and appalled in equal measure as she took in the room. The entire house was red! From the curtains to the sofas, the dining chairs, the cushions and even the cup Naad held in his left hand. Everything was tastefully done, nevertheless, a fiery engine red!

Naad caught her expression and laughed. 'You haven't seen the worst of it. Papa ji was very fond of this colour, so he used it everywhere. I am sort of growing fond of it. Come on,' he beckoned to her. 'Let's talk in my study. Can I offer you tea or coffee?'

She shook her head lightly. 'I'm good, thank you.'

He led her down a passage where an entire wall was devoted to familial, patriarchal portraits. As they walked by, Satyadarshi noticed all the men shared the same middle name and commented on it.

'Do all the Chopra males have the same middle names?'

'Yes, all the men in our family share Rishabh as their middle name. It's a quirk. What can I say?' His shoulders shrugged.

The study was huge, with an entire wall of soundproof glass that muted all the traffic noise effortlessly. Naad sat behind an obsessively neat, gleaming desk and waited until she was seated before speaking.

'So, how can I help you, Ms Satyadarshi?'

'If you don't mind me asking, how did your father die?'

'As I mentioned on the phone, it was a sudden cardiac attack. He was out taking a walk near Haji Ali, on the Lovedale flyover, when he collapsed. It was his morning ritual – he'd jog for forty-five minutes and then start his day at the office. But on that day ... his heart just gave up.' He sighed heavily.

'I'm so sorry to hear that, Mr Chopra. Do you or your father know Ms Laxmi Pancham?'

Naad frowned for a minute and said, 'Can't say I do. Papa ji never mentioned her name. But I could be wrong. I am still coming to terms with his sudden death. Why?'

'It's connected to the case I'm investigating. She was murdered recently, and her son hired me to dig into her death.'

'Ah, the old lady found dead in her room. I read about it in the newspaper. But how's her death related to Papa ji's?'

'Ms Laxmi used to call your father every first Monday of the month, and they would speak for fifteen to twenty minutes each time.'

'Huh ... that's odd. But again, how is it connected to us, Ms Satyadarshi?'

'I'm grasping at straws here. I'd hoped to speak to your father, but that is not possible now. May I take a quick look around his office? Or his bedroom?'

Reading Naad's hesitation, Satyadarshi said, 'I only want to have a look, Mr Chopra. Sometimes, clues just catch one's eye. You can stay with me while I examine the room.'

He mulled it over before nodding. 'Sure, let me take you there.'

The late Mr Chopra's bedroom was so large that Gaiety Theatre might've fit inside, with the popcorn machine too. It had a king-size bed, and its headboards, bed sheets and even duvets were crimson! Everywhere she looked, something vermilion lurked – curtains, cupboard handles, even the commode, visible through the open bathroom door.

How can someone sleep in excess of red?!

Naad's hawk-like gaze seemed to read her mind, and with a laugh, he said, 'I told you, you hadn't seen the worst of it.'

The bedroom, walk-in closet and the bathroom were full of only clothes and toiletries – also red, Satyadarshi noted with a subdued shudder. Naad led her to his father's adjoining office. A rosewood desk dominated the room, blocking a small book rack behind it. She perused the carelessly placed legal books but found nothing connecting Laxmi Pancham to the Chopras. The room was generic. Naad stood watching her but remained silent.

Satyadarshi was about to give up when she spotted the wall hanging. It was almost identical to the one in Laxmi's room!

A cherry-red wall hanging trimmed with red, brown, green, blue and more tassels. At its centre, a seven-pointed star cradled a golden musical note, flanked by a cow and an eagle.

She spun around and retraced her steps to the modest bookshelf. Her sudden quickness surprised and puzzled

Naad. Rummaging among the leather-bound, heavy books, she located what she sought – the same book that had been on Laxmi's shelf.

Too many overlaps. Maybe instinct wasn't leading me into a dead end after all.

'Did your father sing or play an instrument?' Satyadarshi asked.

'No, but he donated tons of money to the Gandharva Institute. Have you heard of it?'

'The Gandharva Mahavidyalaya Mandal that holds the music and dance examinations, right?'

My entire life has passed walking along its corridors!

'The same. The board dedicated a wing of the institute to my father. My sister now oversees the donations after his death.'

She perused the book under Naad's eagle eyes. It was the same book. Or close, a cousin in another cover. Different illustrations, same ending: the Garuda Mantra.

Om Tatpurushay Vidmahe /

Suvarnapakshaya dheemahee /

Tanno Garudah Prachodayat ||

Does the Garuda Mantra refer to the eagle on the wall hanging? How bizarre.

Satyadarshi was beginning to think she hadn't left music behind after all; it had clawed its way back into her life – dressed in blood and metaphor.

5

Once she wrapped up the Chopra visit, Satyadarshi drove onto Maharshi Karve road.

Time to crack the fridge-opening mystery of Mr Baby Bimbette.

It was almost lunchtime, and Satyadarshi debated during the hour-long drive from Worli to Colaba whether she should visit Preia's house before or after grabbing some grub. Her stomach, rumbling at the thought of the green chutney, boiled-and-sliced-potato vegetable sandwich, sealed the decision.

To the soundtrack of 1990s Indi-pop, she cursed and negotiated the pothole-ridden roads, humming along to Shaan's 'Tanha Dil'.

What an era that was!

Finding a parking spot near the Air India office building was pure serendipity. Satyadarshi hopped over to the Famous Sandwich roadside stall.

'Hello, Inspector Madam. You've come to my stall after so long! How many thieves have you snatched off the roads so far?' Raju, the owner, grinned and shook her hand as

Satyadarshi placed her order for a vegetable grilled cheese sandwich.

'Arrey, Raju, I quit the force, remember?' She laughed, waving off his compliment.

'I remember, Madam, but you'll always remind me of the police. Are you here on a case?' His fingers moved expertly over the cutting board as he skipped the pre-cut vegetables and chopped fresh ones for her.

'Yeah, I've got to visit South Bombay on a follow-up.'

Satyadarshi's mouth watered as the steamy aroma of melting cheese hit her senses.

'Here you go, Madam.' Raju offered the grilled delicacy to her.

Biting into the gooey yet crispy sandwich, she blanked out everything else. For that instant, only she and the food on her plate existed – perfectly complementing each other: one meant to satisfy, the other craving satisfaction. She licked her fingers clean once done.

Gone too soon.

After a few more minutes of catching up, Satyadarshi waved goodbye to Raju and headed towards the Famous Juice Centre, a roadside kiosk run by Raju's brother. Grabbing a mixed-fruit cocktail, she slurped her way to her car. After sipping up the last drop of juice through the straw, Satyadarshi pushed her Alto into gear and headed towards Shalaka building for a date with Mr Baby Bimbette.

Appa and Satyadarshi were dog lovers, but Aai had severe allergies to dog dander. Her dreams of being a dog mommy

– or even a dog sibling as a kid – never came true. When her father was around, they would feed the stray dogs living near their building. It was their night-time ritual. Aai ensured they washed their hands once they got home.

Stray dogs are dogs who belong to everyone. All they need is a loving touch, a kind voice, and their hearts are yours forever. Their loyalty remains yours whether you feed them or not. Dogs really are angels on earth, with sharp teeth, somewhat dubious breath and tails.

She reached just in time as the dog walker, Charan, exited the building for their afternoon walk. Baby Bimbette was a fawn-coloured pug whose lustrous fur reflected the sunlight.

His hair is so much better than mine. Shiny and thick.

The pug's beady eyes held a kind expression as his pink tongue lolled in anticipation. Charan held a rainbow-coloured leash in one hand, and a matching backpack was slung over his shoulder, both displaying the logo of an international pet food company.

Satyadarshi decided to stay back and follow them to see how everything played out. Connecting her wireless earphones, she pulled her ponytail through the backstrap of her baseball cap and slipped on her sunglasses. Satyadarshi then folded her lanky body, pretending to re-tie her shoes, aware that the cap hid her face as Charan and his ward walked past.

Baby Bimbette was an overstuffed accordion of a dog, but so ridiculously adorable ... I could kiss him forever!

The man and the dog diligently walked from their building

towards Colaba Causeway, stopping every few metres as people who knew Baby Bimbette petted and cuddled him. The canine greeted each person with a lifetime supply of licks and excited yelps. Several of them offered Parle-G biscuits and other nibbles as treats to the dog, who gobbled them up in a heartbeat, his curled tail waving in appreciation. Even a balding beggar recognized him and offered his meagre food, a few pieces of stale bread, to the pug's delight.

As they finished their one-kilometre walk, Charan withdrew a water bottle and a bowl and offered it to the thirsty dog. On their return journey, a new set of dog lovers fed different bite-sized treats to Baby Bimbette.

No wonder, despite his daily two-kilometre walk, his food intake far outweighs his exercise.

She watched, horrified and impressed, as Baby Bimbette inhaled a full cheese sandwich in three bites.

He reminds me of ... me.

Satyadarshi recorded her findings on her mobile, and Charan and his precious load disappeared into the building.

As she saw the last of the rotund pug, she flushed pink as an image of a future Satyadarshi, waddling sausage-like, seared itself into her mind. She resolved to watch what she ate more carefully and to exercise regularly.

Yoga, here I come! The Baby Bimbette case has left me with a new resolve and a bank account full of money. Time to head home and try to beat the omnipresent traffic.

She hit only four jams on the way back – a miracle in itself. Satyadarshi had just crossed Worli when she received a call from one of Laxmi's friends, the same one who hadn't answered her earlier. She checked for lurking traffic cops before answering the call on her headset.

'I received a call from this number,' a baritone voice greeted her.

'Hello, Mr Suhel Dhaivat.' She said, reading his name off the phone. 'I'm Satyadarshi, an investigator looking into the death of Ms Laxmi Pancham. Is this a good time to talk to you?'

'Yes. Yes, perfect timing. I heard about Laxmi's shocking death. She was my dear friend and partner, and I will miss her dearly. But I think I know why Laxmi was murdered. And the danger is creeping closer to me. I've got a feeling I'm next on the list, beta. That's why I'm going to initiate the next plan of action.'

Huh? Senile or the killer? Initiate what exactly?

'Mr Dhaivat, sir, please listen to me. If you feel you are in danger, lock yourself inside your bedroom and immediately call the police. Don't open the door to anyone. Where do you stay?'

'I stay at B-102, Lotus Colony, behind Nehru Planetarium.'

'Lock yourself in ASAP, sir. I'll be there in fifteen minutes.' *I hope,* she muttered.

Satyadarshi accelerated, testing her shuddering car's limits. Congestion at Thadani Marg set her behind by six minutes.

During peak hours in Bombay, every emergency is a gamble between life and death.

She threw her baseball hat on the seat and rolled her shoulders as her hands curled around the cracked steering wheel cover.

Getting flustered helps no one, Darshi.

She took a deep breath and, on the count of three, exhaled, calming herself down.

Even though I have a few friends left in the police, they can't reach out to help me. They could land in trouble with the higher-ups and get punished. The bridge with my old employer was burnt to ashes ages ago.

What if Mr Dhaivat is really in danger? I need him alive to answer my questions. From the brief conversation we had, I am not exactly sure what's happening, but my gut's telling me to get there quickly.

Could this be how the spider spins the web?

6

After a twenty-four-minute delay that felt like an hour, Satyadarshi reached B-102. The door was ajar. Too ajar.

Why didn't he lock it?

Hesitantly, she called out, pushing her purse strap back on her shoulder – it kept slipping off.

'Mr Suhel?' she raised her voice. 'Sir, we spoke over the phone a while back. I'm the PI, Satyadarshi.'

A sense of foreboding enveloped her; the hair on the back of her neck bristled as she stood in the passage, facing the open door. A shadow lunged at her. Before she could react, she was shoved inside the apartment and the entrance slammed shut. As it happened, she caught a glimpse of a gloved hand wearing a black Titan watch pushing her inside.

Satyadarshi yelped as she hit her shoulder against the door jamb and her bag's strap snagged on the knob, tearing it apart. Her outstretched hands dashed into a table, and she clutched it for support.

The door bolt slid into place with an ominous click as she sprinted back towards it. Satyadarshi tried to pull the door, but it wouldn't budge.

She was locked in the apartment. From the outside.

What in the world is going on? This feels like a trap, and I walked right in.

She rubbed her sore shoulder and rotated her arm to get some feeling back. Satyadarshi waited until her eyes adjusted to the darkness, loath to touch anything. With her heartbeat echoing in her ears, she sidestepped her way deeper into the flat. Withdrawing a pen from her bag, she flipped several switches before finding the one that covered the room in a fluorescent light.

The floor creaked under her steps. *Could another intruder still be around?*

Satyadarshi edged forward, every nerve on alert. *I miss the days when I used to carry a gun. I really need to apply for a permit again. Aai would have a coronary.*

She entered the tidy kitchen where the remnants of tea – a single cup, saucepan, spoon and sieve – had been washed and placed to dry on the black counter.

Nothing here.

Her empty stomach let out a loud rumble, startling her. She was hungry after the tiny sandwich and juice, but now wasn't the time to think about food.

'Mr Dhaivat? Are you okay?' The curtains rustled in the mild breeze, but otherwise silence reigned.

Where is the man? Could he have lured me here? Why? Why am I locked in this house? I've got more questions than answers.

The solitary bedroom captured her attention as soon as she entered.

No one is around.

A wall hanging was displayed over the bed. Her pulse hadn't settled, but curiosity momentarily overrode fear.

It was identical to the ones she had seen in Laxmi's and Chopra's respective rooms, with one notable difference – this one blazed yellow. A seven-pointed star encircled a golden musical note, with a horse and an eagle on either side. Tassels in red, gold, white, blue and other bright colours swung from its edge.

A large figurine of Lord Ganesha in his father Shiva's classic Natarajan pose, graced the side table. The bed was made and undisturbed, with the bed sheet pulled tightly against the mattress.

Mr Dhaivat's bedroom appears untouched.

She spotted the bathroom door and trudged towards it, the pit in her stomach sinking to her knees, then plummeting to her feet. Using her right toe to nudge it further, she noticed the door jamb was splintered near the lock, with broken wooden shards scattered on the floor.

Stepping inside, she spotted a body crumpled on the floor next to the white commode. An old man lay face-up, eyes staring at the yellow wall in front of him – a wall he couldn't see anymore. There was a bullet hole in his forehead, the surrounding skin singed black. The metallic tang of blood mixed with gunpowder assailed her nostrils.

Satyadarshi closed her eyes and took a shaky breath. Calming her mind, she forced them open, relying on her training.

She knew her time was limited; she had a lot to do before the police arrived. And they would. Someone would have called them in. *Maybe the killer himself.*

She donned a pair of ever-ready sterile gloves from her purse as she stepped closer to the supine body and snapped several photographs with her mobile. Pressing her lips together as she leaned in to take close-up shots, avoiding the blood pooling on the creamy lemon-coloured bathroom floor, she shoved her feelings aside.

Rising, she replaced the phone in her single-strapped bag and ferreted around but found nothing of importance in the cabinets.

With a last look around, Satyadarshi jumped back into the bedroom and scrutinized it.

I should find the same Origin of Music Across Indian Temples *book here if my gut feeling is correct. Where can it be? I don't know why, but I feel the book holds the key.*

She checked the double-door cupboards, brushing her hands under the neatly ironed shirts. Satyadarshi ran her fingers down the trousers that hung from the bar, hoping to find something. Anything. The side table contained just an old MTNL telephone book, a relic of the past, and several cobwebs, while the mattress hid no secrets underneath it.

Mr Dhaivat's bedroom yielded zilch. Frustrated, she checked the time on her watch.

Hurry, Darshi, hurry.

With time ticking, she dashed to the kitchen and rummaged through the pots, pans, jars and boxes.

Empty.

The turmeric-coloured light of a tiny yet intricately carved marble temple caught her attention, and she approached it. The small drawer slid open at Satyadarshi's touch, revealing the *Bhagwad Gita* and other prayer books. She riffled through the *Gita* but saw in its pages only a dwindling chance of knowledge or salvation for herself.

Satyadarshi picked up an unusually thick *Ganesh Aarti* book next. Nestled between its pages lay the elusive book. She was just about to examine it when an urgent knock on the door interrupted her. Each version of the book seemed tuned to its owner.

'Open up! It's the police.'

Startled, she fumbled and dropped the book.

Sloppy. Dammit.

She picked it up, tucked it inside the waistband of her black trousers and pulled her paisley-printed shirt out. Taking several deep breaths, she opened the door, which swung easily once the latches on the outside were undone.

Trust the Bombay police to come on time when not wanted. Someone from the society must've seen me being shoved in.

After a harrowing time at the Mahalaxmi police station – where a near-arrest was avoided only because no gunpowder residue was found on her hands, and thanks to her previous stint as an inspector in the Colaba division – Satyadarshi was released with a warning. She had to eat a humble pie, thanking the inspector-in-charge profusely and tolerating his misogynistic comments on women detectives.

'Let the real cops handle the murder' rankled her, but she wasn't in a position to argue or even roll her eyes. In the whole melee, she had managed to slip the slim book into her favourite – though now-damaged – handbag, where it settled amongst the debris of paraphernalia she carried every day.

If only I had left the station with my reputation intact. Well, either my dignity or my reputation could have been salvaged – not both.

She reached home exhausted, her mind birthing more questions than it could hold.

All my leads are turning into dead ends. Literally. The only clue – a tenuous one at best – is the music book.

But will it sing like the nightingale?

⁂

The man lay in shavasana, forcing his body to relax. His brain raced as fast as his body slowed. He ignored the spiky dried leaves under his bare back – acupressure needles from nature, pressing sharp reminders into his skin.

The old man had held on for a surprisingly long time, despite the pressure he'd applied. Just like that insufferable Laxmi. Steel-spined, both of them. But not strong enough to survive the onslaught.

And it had been an onslaught.

When he struck Suhel in the solar plexus and watched the doddering fool bend over in pain, it was only his innate sense of caution that stopped him from hitting him again. In the end, the old man did reveal secrets.

Loose lips sink ships.

That thought bloomed bright and clear as he pulled the trigger. The bitter tang of nitroglycerine smarted his eyes and nostrils. The smell of an ending.

The only blip in his perfect execution was the chit of a girl's unexpected arrival.

Why was she there? Was she tracking me?

By trying to mend ways with her, he thought he had dodged a bullet. Her presence had thrown him off his game, and only quick thinking – shoving her inside the apartment – had saved him. Otherwise, it would have been game over for him.

Well, his luck had held, and it had all played out perfectly.

Six down and one to go. And that one I will enjoy the most.

Om visvaaya naam /

Gandharvalochni naami lousatikarnai /

Tasmai vishwaya swaha ||

At the 1000th recitation, his eyes snapped open, and he stared at the thick foliage in front of him. It blurred as his mind conjured the face of his next enemy – their name, their soon to-be agonizing final moments.

The last would be the most challenging one. The most personal.

The man could almost visualize the gold-plated exterior walls of the old temple as the first rays of the sun hit them.

One couldn't look at them without squinting in the blinding glare. The statue of Lord Vishnu resting under the canopy of the five-hooded Anantha was a sight to behold. But it wasn't the majestic Anantha Sayanam posture that made his heart race.

In his mind, the temple doors screeched open, ancient hinges wailing at the disturbance. Inside, the treasure shimmered – a delirium of gold, centuries hoarded, waiting for him. Shining only for him. He was the axis they circled, the earth that gave their light meaning. Their brilliance pulsed for him alone, and it made him deliriously happy – happy knowing that *he* had completed the task countless others had failed to finish.

He was the one who cracked the Naag Paasam Mantra.

The one who tamed the snakes.

He wasn't just a man.

He was the mighty eagle, the mighty Garuda. The destroyer of snakes.

At the heart of it, he was the one with all the knowledge. Not just Saraswati Devi's disciple, but the composer of a new Veda – one born of fire and blood.

The man who knew everything.

A smile crept across his face as he sat up, the leaves rustling, to start the Dashansh Havan. The final offering before victory was in his grasp. Everything was ready – the ghee, the havan ingredients, the matchsticks, the flowers, the Glock handgun lying on a yellow cloth. Everything was perfect.

Even the forest abutting Aarey Milk Colony – his usual hideout – stayed silent today, as if encouraging him. People feared the place, calling it haunted, but he had formed a kinship with it. The lonely forest matched him, beat for beat. Dark, full of secrets and without an iota of fear. Like him.

The choice of this isolated quasi-jungle is perfect. No one will disturb me here. Or notice the smoke trails.

He anointed the gun with a red kumkum tilak and patted it with reverence. It had done its job well. He lit the match, and the dry wood instantly caught fire, starting with a hiss. As he poured a spoonful of ghee into the now smouldering fire, he began chanting.

He'd learnt the Stambhan Mantra from the Rudrayamala Tantra, meant to bind the enemy's mind. Chanted 108 times, it was said to cloud reason and steal the will to fight.

He was only nine chants in.

Just ninety-nine to go.

Each one drawing him nearer to the silence that would follow the last breath.

7

Satyadarshi woke up feeling exhausted. Fortunately, she had remembered to draw the curtains over the windows before she crashed last night. Even though their building didn't lie on the arterial road, the occasional spluttering of autos and the hissing of the bikes were potential sleep destroyers.

Last night's events kept tumbling in her mind, like lint trapped in a washing machine. Like a whoosh of air escaping a balloon, she deflated against the headboard, clutching her rainbow-coloured bed sheet. Images of Suhel Dhaivat's crumpled body had haunted her the entire night, and she was probably going to struggle with them throughout the day.

Unless something else happens. No, think positive, Darshi. Maybe I can manifest something good, like Twarita keeps harping on about.

Despite her stint as a police inspector, it was always difficult for her to see dead bodies – especially when one came so close to the killer, his gloved hand had even touched her!

If only I hadn't got stuck in the jam, I could've saved Mr Dhaivat's life and caught the killer. If only ...

She was rubbing her face, willing away the tiredness, when Ragini walked into her room carrying a wooden tray with a teakettle and Satyadarshi's favourite mug. It was a ceramic, multicoloured mug that Ajji had gifted her a few years before she died. At its centre, a meditating figure sat cross-legged – serene, eyes closed, palms up in perfect mudra – while a chaotic swirl of cartoon traffic horns, autorickshaws, honking cars and tiny scooters zoomed around like flies. A glowing halo behind the figure was shaped like a traffic signal. Underneath it a stylized caption read: 'Inner peace loading ... buffering ... stuck in Mumbai traffic.'

It was a running joke between her grandmother and Satyadarshi, and Ajji always teased her that peace was overrated and patience a scam; that Satyadarshi wasn't impatient, she just didn't think before jumping. She hadn't been very close to her grandmother, but they'd had their moments. And Ragini often lamented that Satyadarshi's stubborn streak came from her Ajji, who could outstare a mirror and win.

The cup's cheeky text usually made her smile, but today she wasn't in the mood. She forced herself to shrug off the black cloud that hung around her, lest it invite another lecture from her mother. Ragini placed the tray on the coffee table and flung the curtains open. The 7:00 a.m. sun flirted with the trees outside, casting dancing shadows on the walls and the mosaic-tiled floor.

'I knew you'd had a late and probably disturbing evening, so I thought I'd get a pot of tea for my beautiful and hard-working daughter,' said Ragini, sitting on the edge of the bed. She caressed Satyadarshi's head with delicate, butterfly-like movements, massaging her forehead and running her fingers through her daughter's long hair.

Peering into her mother's guileless eyes, so similar to her own, Satyadarshi's antennae immediately sprung to attention. A memory bubbled up – of Aai's touch whenever she scraped her knee as a kid. But this current avatar of Aai had something up her sleeve. This was no comforting touch, it was more like a prelude to a favour.

'That'll be awesome. A cup of tea will definitely help me,' she mumbled.

'Of course it will. Tea fixes almost everything.' A brief smile flitted across Ragini's face. She fidgeted with the edge of a crocheted pillow, twirling a loose thread around her index finger. 'How's your work schedule today?'

The humming antennae buzzed with vigour. 'My work schedule? Why? I have to dictate the Baby Bimbette case report to Twa, in addition to yesterday's events,' groaned Satyadarshi.

'Baby Bimbetter? A new restaurant?' Ragini's eyebrows danced the samba across her forehead.

'A social media influencer hired me for a case to follow her pug as he was piling on weight.'

'Is the lady's name Baby Bimbetter? Tsk, a few people need a shot of self-esteem in their arms. Or brains.' Ragini tittered.

'Hah. No, though you aren't far off the mark, Aai. It's her dog's name. And it's Baby Bimbette.'

Ragini rolled her eyes. 'Big difference – Bimbette or Bimbetter. As if either one makes more sense. Anyhow, would you be free for a few hours in the morning?'

'Depends.' *On what you want me to do, dearest always-up-to-tricks mother.*

'Well. Do you remember my school friend, Vaijanthi?' At Satyadarshi's nod, Ragini continued. 'Her son, Jai, you remember him? He's almost as old as you, and he's moved here from Pune, changing jobs. Jai's pursuing his PhD on some strange topic about old temples. No, wait! I made myself remember – haan, his topic is on King Ashoka's dynasty.'

Ragini beamed at her daughter, pleased with her recall. 'Vaiju called yesterday and wondered if you could show Jai around. He doesn't know anyone here, na?'

'Oh, Aai. I hope this isn't one of your matchmaking attempts with Vaiju Aunty. It's very annoying and demeaning that my mother has to resort to finding boyfriends for me,' said Satyadarshi, her eyes flashing.

'Haw, Darshi. You're such an evil child.' She waved her hand dismissively. 'And I don't look for ... ' She made air quotes. ' ... "potential boyfriends", but life partners for my only child. After the fiasco last time, I dare not arrange anything for fear of being ostracized by society.'

'Well, the "suitable boy" you chose was selling weed. Was high on it, too.'

Ragini shrugged. 'I thought he had bedroom eyes.'

Satyadarshi snorted.

'What? He had such dreamy eyes!' A goofy smile played on her lips. 'They reminded me of Aamir Khan's eyes.'

'Stoner's eyes, more like it. Aamir Khan's eyes never sold me hash brownies, Aai, but whatever. What am I expected to do with Jai?'

'Whatever you can.'

Satyadarshi shook her head at Ragini's naughty expression. 'Okay,' a sigh escaped her. 'Will a meeting at 10 suit him?'

Ragini rubbed her hands with glee. 'I guess so. Also, can you wear the pink chikankari salwar kameez? You look so beautiful in it.'

'Don't push it, Aai.'

The turquoise facade of the Jamjar Diner on Hill Road beckoned Satyadarshi. Winking at the familiar figure manning the front desk, she reached across his table to swipe two Phantom sweet cigarettes and a few Kismi toffees from the tall mason jars that were filled to capacity.

I can ease this ordeal with candy.

As the Phantom cigarette melted in her mouth, she relished its sweet aftertaste. In protest, she had worn the dullest outfit in her wardrobe – a frayed pair of khaki trousers and a green button-down shirt. Her hair was braided and swung down her back. Her favourite handbag – or 'hold-all', as Ragini called it – pulled down on her shoulder, its weight both grounding and familiar. Ragini had fixed its strap last night.

I look like I'm here to deliver a parcel. All that's missing is an olive-green satchel. But at least this will ensure Jai gets no romantic ideas. Unless he's into postwomen or into postal fashion. That would be a plot twist.

She immediately spotted a single guy dressed in faded blue jeans and a white shirt. He stared at the table mat as if trying to decipher its hidden message. His long legs stretched out in front of him, and he awkwardly tried to fold and unfold them under the table. A lock of wavy hair fell across his forehead, and his long fingers struggled to keep it in place.

Satyadarshi observed him, hidden in the shadows, before walking in his direction.

'Jai? Hello, I'm Satyadarshi. It's nice to meet you.' *I'd rather face a firing squad. Hush now, snarky mind.*

Jai, startled by her sudden appearance, tried to stand up but banged both knees against the table as he held onto it for balance. She winced at the resounding painful thud. *That's going to hurt later.*

Satyadarshi held her hand out. Jai grasped it after a brief delay, shaking it firmly, while maintaining eye contact. He held onto her hands for a tad bit longer than necessary, and his eyes lingered on her crooked tooth, christened 'Sleuthing Fang' by Twarita. Appa used to say she always carried a piece of her beloved dogs with her – a sharp canine – much to Ragini's chagrin, who wanted her to wear braces.

Satyadarshi smiled wider at him, and he smiled back.

Good handshaker. Nice long … hands, too. She bit her lip to stop smiling at her own joke.

'Hello, Satyadarshi. First, let me thank you for taking the time out of a working day. I know it's not easy.' His deep baritone voice reminded her of Jagjit Singh singing ghazals – soulful, like Jai's brown eyes with thick lashes.

Now those are a pair of bedroom eyes. Not to mention that cleft-y chin.

'Not a problem. Have you ordered yet?' she asked, and Jai shook his head. 'Do you eat eggs? Great.'

Satyadarshi beckoned the server over. 'Two Full Monties,' she said. Jai chuckled as she continued, 'One with baked beans and the other with potato wedges. One hot chocolate with marshmallows. And,' she raised an eyebrow at Jai, who responded with 'Cappuccino.'

Satyadarshi clapped her hands. 'Good, now that's out of the way. So, Jai, what do you do besides, I hope not, jaywalking?'

His laughter is like warm honey dripping onto one's palm … Stop it!

'My work and the PhD keep me pretty busy.'

'I can imagine. Actually, I can't. How do you find time to study after a full day of work?'

'Oh, I've got no social life. Absolutely zero. So, it's straight home after work to write, and my weekends are spent in the library, researching. My topic's rather offbeat.'

Satyadarshi nodded. *Nerd alert. Aai sure knows how to pick them. Those eyes, though.*

'Aai mentioned your dissertation's on Indian history.'

It appeared as if a light switch was flicked on, and Jai's entire face lit up from the inside. The cleft in his chin deepened, and his shoulders seemed to get wider as he sat up straight. Satyadarshi's attention was held by the lush lips, and she missed his opening sentence.

' ... mainly about King Ashoka and his seven unknown men. People assume secret societies like the Knights Templar, Opus Dei or the Freemasons existed only in the West and India was never privy to them.'

'Interesting. Dan Brown made them famous.' *Where is the food?*

'Oh, yes. Especially when you understand the intelligence and planning behind them. King Ashoka, too, had his own secret society – seven branches, each associated with a field of science: statistics, warfare, chemistry, et cetera.'

Satyadarshi let loose a smile. *Seriously, where IS the food?*

'Especially after the massive losses at the Kalinga battle, Ashoka formed a covert group. He was ahead of his time and didn't bother with gender rules; both men and women were chosen to lead the groups.'

Aai needs payback for making me put up with this ... good-looking yap-machine and his lecturing-yet-delicious lips.

'To keep them a secret, Ashoka devised a way to hide them in plain sight. And this idea caught on, and several kings later used the septet's services to hide their treasures.' Jai stopped mid-sentence. 'Sorry, I sound like a podcast. It's just rare to meet someone who doesn't yawn when I say "Ashoka".' A sheepish smile appeared on his face.

'No, it's pretty cool. Our ancestors were pretty much sorted. Unlike us.'

'That they were. But enough about me.' His eyes latched onto hers. 'Tell me about yourself. Amma told me you left the police force to start your detective agency?'

'Yeah. Police work didn't pan out in the way I'd imagined. Private detecting is definitely more tedious – with a quarter of the resources and force of the police – but it has its moments.'

'I can imagine. Actually, I can't.'

The nerd has a sense of humour.

Satyadarshi acknowledged the comment with a nod, just as the sound of the newspaper rustling in the opposite booth caught her attention. The man there flipped his paper, and the headline 'Vault B' jumped out at her. *Idiots were still trying to break the seal. Of course they were.*

'I can't believe people are still trying to open that temple's famous room,' she said, gesturing towards the newspaper.

Jai turned to peek. 'Yes. Vault B – the one with the intertwined snakes on the last door. The Travancore king also relied on the services of the septet ... '

Satyadarshi remembered Ajoba's old book on forgotten Indian inventions – how his eyes twinkled when he'd said, 'We were geniuses, before we became obedient.'

' ... to safeguard the treasures inside the temple he constructed. He designed it in such a way that the Naag

Bandhan on the door could be broken only if one recited, at the right pitch and frequency, the … '

Jai's verbal diarrhoea was cut short as the waiter arrived with their food and interrupted their conversation. The heady aroma of cocoa wafted into her nostrils. *It'll be alright, Darshi! Hot chocolate is the solution to everything.*

'Wow, this looks good!' exclaimed Jai, eyeing the fluffy omelette with the side of baked beans arranged artfully on the kitschy crockery.

'Wait until you taste it. It's sublime.' Jai's ecstatic expression proved her right.

While eating, Jai addressed the elephant in the room. He touched her hand briefly. 'There's something I want to set straight. Amma and your mother have been childhood friends, and they have this entire idea of you and me getting together from the time we were kids. I've tried and failed to warn Amma against it, but she's resilient. I just don't want you to feel awkward about this meeting or forced to "show me around". I can manage that myself, but Amma just doesn't get it.'

She laughed, waving her fork in the air. 'Tell me about it. Aai keeps setting me up on these "dates" with soul-sucking, boring men. Sometimes I think it's a ploy, so that when they finally ask the two of us to meet, we'd find each other interesting. Vaiju Aunty can't be as bad as Aai. Aai is relentless. She even tried to set me up with a client once. Phew, that was awkward.'

'I get it. So, let's just enjoy each other's company and thwart all their plans, yeah?'

'Deal.'

Finally. Someone who understands the helicopter mom pressures.

Satyadarshi was pleased to find that their conversation flowed well after the initial hiccups.

Jai's an interesting nerd until he starts to yap about his PhD. I wouldn't mind meeting him again. Ashoka and his seven unknowns can't solve my case even if they tried.

8

Satyadarshi reached the office late, waving at Twarita, who was – as always – on the phone, taking notes. After breakfast with the nerdy but funny Jai, she had caught a local from Bandra to Dadar, then cabbed it to Sion, reaching by noon. Several missed calls from her father blinked on her phone, and she wondered what he wanted as she plonked into her chair.

On the wall opposite her desk hung a family photograph taken in happier times, before Appa had grown a French beard. She occasionally wondered how her parents ended up together, given they came from not only different mindsets but different states.

Aai, unlike most steady, practical Maharashtrians, was almost a free spirit – whimsical and practical in equal parts, depending on her mood, despite her strict mother. Appa, on the other hand, was a proper stick-in-the-mud kind of man. Even his wardrobe followed a schedule, fixed by the day of the week, though it was always a varied hue of blue-chequered shirts with jeans.

I wonder how he wore a traditional outfit for their wedding. Aai must have exhausted all her wiles to convince him.

In the snapshot, her father, Raghuram, stood tall and upright, flanked by Ragini and Satyadarshi, his arms encircling the two women who leaned into him. His Titan watch – the black one he never took off except for baths – rested on her shoulder as the photo-version of Satyadarshi gazed up at him, laughing.

The hand that had pushed me into Mr Suhel Dhaivat's house yesterday had also worn a black Titan watch. Yeah, it's a very popular watch, so nothing there. Could there be something? No, it's Appa! The photograph, however, tugged a reluctant smile from her before it receded.

I never thought they'd split. I'll return his calls later. I need to solve Laxmi's case fast to earn the bonus.

Settling in, she dragged her mind out of nostalgia and concentrated on the problem at hand. She placed the three books – two borrowed, one flicked – on her table and examined them. All the dog-eared books, worn to variable degrees, resembled each other like cousins at a wedding.

Each book featured a different Ragamala illustration: intricate miniature paintings, where ragas and raginis were personified as men, women or divine figures. Sometimes as lovers in a palace courtyard, sometimes as ascetics in meditation. The paintings varied by region and style, reflecting different moods, seasons and even times of day associated with each raga.

The only commonality across all three copies was on the last page: a precise rendering of the Garuda Mantra.

Om Tatpurushay Vidmahe /

Suvarnapakshaya dheemahee /

Tanno Garudah Prachodayat ||

That part hadn't changed – which made her deeply suspicious.

Her chin sank into her palm, the case fading again as memories flooded her.

Bhairavi Ajji weaving intricate bandishes with no effort, stitching different ragas together, making it seem seamless. Ajoba, singing in the higher octaves, would often join her. The music room would reverberate – shimmer – with their voices. It felt like a fusion of talent so pure, so reverential, they made us feel each sur, each bhav, each note. Even Dhrupad Mama, ever the grump, would drop his surly expression and soften his frown. That was until Aai joined the duo – then the three, similar, yet uniquely distinct voices blended into one raga.

Satyadarshi then reprimanded herself. *This is a great time meandering down memory lane, Darshi, but how does this tie in with Laxmi Pancham and her friends' deaths?*

Her gaze dropped back to the volume. *And why does the Garuda Mantra keep cropping up? What can I recollect about it? Why was it recited?*

Appa's voice surfaced in her mind, smooth and certain. 'It wards off the fear of snakes,' he had once said, his fingers moving over the jaap mala.

But none of the three people were bitten by snakes. Appa said it's also meant to ward off negative energies, overcome diseases and cure poisonous bites. Snakes. Where did I hear about them recently?

Shaking off the thought, she flipped open her laptop. Updating the entry under Suhel Dhaivat, she re-read her notes.

Out of the six numbers on Laxmi's final call list, she had traced two of them – Mr Chopra and Mr Dhaivat – both dead before she could interrogate them. She looked at the other names: Mr Shadaj, Mr Gandhar, Mr Raag and Ms Madhyama. As per their mobile records, their phones had been inactive for weeks.

Tapping a pen against her chin, she missed the arrival of Twarita, who placed a cup of steaming cutting chai and four vada pavs in front of her.

'Good afternoon, SD. After hearing about your day yesterday, I scurried over to the Jumbo Vada Pav to fetch these. I even remembered to get the extra fried chillies and your favourite red garlic chutney.'

'Hey! How did *you* hear about my day yesterday?'

'Hello?' Twarita waved the fried snack in front of her. 'Why do you forget that I'm still friends with the police, unlike you, bridge-burning boss lady? And after your arrest ... '

'I was *not* arrested!'

'Potato, potahto. So, after your *almost*-arrest, the grapevine lit up like Diwali patakhas. Smelt just as good, too. I heard Tamble laid into you about the virtues of letting the "real cops handle murder" and how "delicate hands like yours look good holding a rolling pin and not pistols or shackled in handcuffs".'

Her laughter washed away the residual feelings of Satyadarshi's shame and anger. And she finally saw the humour in it.

'Well, my sheer stupidity led to that torturous diatribe,' she said, picking up a pav, smearing it with the red chutney and replacing the vada. Biting into it, she groaned with pleasure. 'And I know who filled your ears with gossip – your lover boy, Prateek!'

'Prateek is *not* my lover boy!' Twarita spoke through clenched teeth. 'And even if he is, so what?'

Satyadarshi raised her hands in surrender. 'Nothing, baba. I'm sure he's a great guy! In fact, I know he's a great guy – I trained him.' Changing the subject, she added, 'To avoid Aai's lectures, I skipped breakfast, which was probably oats khichdi. That darned thing looks like regurgitated vomit and tastes exactly like how you'd expect it to!' She shuddered.

'But I gorged at the Jamjar Diner with another of Aai's *meet-prospective-hubby-boy*. Remind me to tell you about him. The man wouldn't shut up about Ashoka.'

'King Ashoka?'

'The same.'

'What a weirdo.'

Twarita nibbled on her snack, shaking her head as she saw Satyadarshi wolf one down and reach for another. Mid-bite, Satyadarshi paused and placed the vada pav down.

'Must be something important for you to stop eating after

guzzling down the obviously heavy breakfast you had a few hours back,' smirked Twarita.

'Whatever. I had a radical thought. While Googling the last four names on Laxmi's list, I couldn't find any relevant information about them. And the lack of mobile activity on their numbers churns my gut. Can you tap into your "relevant grapevine" and get any details about them?'

'Of course. As soon as I finish my tea. I'll earn the big bucks you clearly don't pay me.'

After Twarita left to do her thing, Satyadarshi leaned back in her chair, her mind abuzz as she glanced at the three books stacked in the corner.

All this talk of musical theory made her miss her grandfather.

If Ajoba were still around, I'd pick his brain about what connects those notations scribbled in the books and murder. His and Ajji's too. God, sometimes I almost forget about her, Ajoba was always my go-to person. I hope Aai can't tune into my thoughts, or she'd annihilate me.

She remembered how her grandmother, a living legend of the Jaipur Gharana, had kicked up a musical storm by passing the baton to her husband – a man. The gharana purists had balked, enraged that a matrilineal tradition had been broken by the one who had nurtured it. Their house, too, had practically split down the middle, Dhrupad Mama opposing the decision and Aai supporting it.

But Ajji had stood her ground, and Ajoba – with his legit classical credentials and rare gift of singing in both octaves

– had smoothed the discord, like the deft raga transitions he was known for.

A chuckle shot out of her mouth like a bullet. *Memory is such a weird muscle – random, and so very ajeeb.*

Getting back on track, she tapped the books before her, her long fingers with short nails dancing on the covers.

Ajji's Jaipur Gharana fame made her wonder – *could music kill?*

No, that's preposterous.

Still, the case was intricately connected to music – names, notations, books, mantras, ragas.

What connects murder to music – besides their starting alphabets?

9

'Out of the four names you gave me,' Twarita said, bursting into the room and waving a sheet of paper. Her cat-like hazel eyes – a feature they both shared – shone with excitement. 'One is AWOL, and the other three? All dead. Under sort-of suspicious conditions.' She arched her eyebrow. 'All three.'

'Mr Gandhar lived with his wife in Mahim and was found with his head bashed in. His wife, out to buy vegetables, came home to find her husband sprawled on the floor.'

She checked her notes. 'Mr Shadaj was stabbed. He survived but is in a coma – his kids might pull the plug soon. Maybe even this week.'

She raised her hands in a sign of victory. 'The last name on the list, Ms Madhyama, was found in her garden in Dombivli. She was garrotted with a wire trellis that once supported a tomato plant in her vegetable patch. None of the cases had any witnesses, at least none who've stepped forward.'

Twarita slumped into the visitor's chair and raked a hand through her hair, but the layered tresses fell right back into place around her angular face. 'Phew! Did I do good, SD?'

Satyadarshi beamed. 'Twa, you rock. If there's any information that needs extraction, you're my girl.'

Twarita flashed a dazzling smile and shrugged. 'What can I say, SD? You're lucky to have me on your team.'

'And you're lucky to have Prateek in yours,' Satyadarshi mumbled under her breath.

'Hey, I heard that!'

Satyadarshi raised her hands in mock surrender. 'You're the best, Twa. You know what a smart Alec I am!'

Twarita rolled her eyes, mollified. 'The entire world knows that. No one better than your ex-boss in the police!'

Satyadarshi waved the quip away, getting back to business. 'Is there any way that I can meet their families?'

'Hmm, I'll have to cajole their addresses out of my sources. Why do you want to know?'

Satyadarshi held one of the *Origin of Music Across Indian Temples* volumes. 'I want to see if they have a copy of this text in their respective houses. Among other information.'

'Let me get on it. But realistically, that's possible only by late evening when Prateek's shift starts.'

'No worries, I'll schedule an appointment for tomorrow. Today Bombay's humidity is at an all-time high!'

'SD … you know it's Mumbai now.'

Satyadarshi blinked, caught off guard. 'Haan, I know. I keep forgetting. Ajoba always said Bombay. Aai too. It just slips out before I can stop it.'

Twarita smirked. 'You're supposed to be the sharp one, remember?'

Satyadarshi chuckled, then her voice softened. 'For me, Bombay *is* childhood – concerts at Shanmukhananda, Ajoba's hand in mine, the smell of cutting chai at Churchgate. Bombay is a lost melody I still hum occasionally. Mumbai … ' she paused, eyes clouding, 'Mumbai is where I grew up again – case files, late nights, crime scenes. Maybe it's just my own map, not the city's. But sometimes, I'm not sure which version of it I belong to.'

Twarita looked at her, half-teasing, half-gentle. 'Only you could make geography sound like a break-up.'

Satyadarshi smiled faintly, the nostalgia not quite loosening its grip. 'Maybe it *is* a break-up with whom I was. But some names stick to your tongue like old songs … or like a maiden name. Bombay's one of them.'

⌘

Mrs Neela Gandhar was a woman with a slight build. Her eyes bore telltale dark circles, and her glabella gleaned a few tones lighter than the rest of her face. An empty circle where a bindi once lived still claimed its space. She sat daintily on the honey-polished wooden sofa, clutching her phone so tightly her knuckles turned white against it. The sight reminded Satyadarshi of an injured sparrow – her beige sari forming the plumage.

Photographs of the Gandhar family hung on the wall opposite the sofa, where they sat. They chronicled the life of a modest nuclear family – from the couple's wedding to the birth of their children and later, their marriages. At the centre of the tawny hued wall was a garlanded picture of Mr Gandhar, smiling toothily at them through the sparkling glass.

The house was so compact that a sigh would ricochet three times within its tiny two-BHK, but it was spotless, especially the blonde yellow fabric of the couch. Mrs Gandhar clearly took pride in her house and it showed. A straw-coloured Samsung fridge divided the kitchen and the hall where they sat. Three chairs faced the modest television, above which hung a framed photograph of Radha–Krishna. The older woman had placed two cups of tea and a bowl of moong dal namkeen on the centre table.

'The last words my husband said to me were, "Make sure the tendlis are soft but not squishy." And when I came home … ' A shudder ran through her frail body, like a dried leaf cracking in the wind. ' … I found him gone. He loved green leafy vegetables. And tendlis. I can never look at one again. If I'd known this was going to happen, I would've never left him alone. The vegetables cost me my entire life. And they had a special discount going on, too.'

Neela broke down, copious tears tracing rivulets down her papery cheeks. Satyadarshi leaned in to embrace her. She could feel the old lady's brittle bones quivering through the hug.

'Shall I get you a glass of water, Mrs Gandhar?' she asked.

'No, beta.' Neela patted her hand. 'I've got to get used to my husband's aching absence. Why don't you have tea?' She waited until Satyadarshi picked up a cup. 'Did you have some work with us ... with me? Did he know you?' Her sparse hair, tied in a bun, had come undone, and her pinkish scalp shone through as she scrambled to re-tie it.

'No, Madam. I'm a private investigator, and a case brought your husband's death to my attention.' She continued hastily as she saw a frown forming on the older woman's forehead. 'He was friends with Ms Laxmi, whose son hired me.'

'Laxmi Pancham? Oh, yes. She was a dear friend, and her murder was very upsetting for us, especially Gandhar ji. I didn't know Hariesh had hired a private detective. Aren't the police looking into her murder?'

So, Mr Gandhar and Ms Pancham knew each other. How deep did this circle go? she thought.

'They're looking into it, but Mr Pancham was not convinced of their ... ability, or interest, in apprehending her killer. Actually, Mr Gandhar spoke to Ms Laxmi about a fortnight before her death. Would you have any idea about what they discussed?'

'I know how Hariesh feels. The police aren't doing much about my husband's murder either. We are old, so no one bothers about us anymore.' Her bony shoulders moved in a small shrug, tacitly accepting their situation. 'I remember Laxmi called my husband on the day he died, and as soon as he saw her name on the mobile, he sent me out to buy vegetables.' She shook her head. 'He didn't want me to overhear their conversation. Sometimes, Gandhar ji was very secretive. He wouldn't let me sit in the same room when he spoke to certain friends. One of them was Laxmi.'

'Didn't you ask him why? Were you not curious?'

'Not really. Women of my generation didn't cross-question like you girls can do nowadays. We took everything lying down. Though a few times I did catch snippets of their closing conversations, bits about temple vaults and sur-taal. Occasionally, it'd be about an incident that happened in their past, but I don't know the details.

'Whenever Gandhar ji requested me to leave him alone, I'd exit the room and turn on the television. The reruns of *Mahabharata* and *Ramayana* were always playing, and I loved watching them. Radhe Radhe.' She joined her hands and bowed her head.

Satyadarshi whipped out her tattered copy of the music book. 'Neela ji, did Mr Gandhar possess a copy of this book?'

Neela peered at the book, pushing her slipping glasses up until till they kissed her eyebrows. 'I don't know, beta. I'm not into reading books, only magazines. But you can check the rack.' She pointed to the dining area, where in a niche, stood a cane bookshelf crammed with books.

Satyadarshi excused herself and walked over, navigating around the two-person dining table. The slim volume leapt out almost immediately, nestled next to a stack of albums. It was in pristine condition, unlike the other copies.

Knowing what she would find, she turned to the last page.

The Garuda Mantra.

'Pops up again,' she said under her breath.

Next to the shelf, half-hidden behind wooden dining chairs, hung a brown wall hanging. Satyadarshi had almost expected it. The now-familiar seven-pointed star ringed a golden musical note. On either side, a goat and an eagle leaned in as if mid-peck. Tassels in red, gold, white, blue and other bright shades swayed from it.

'Can you hand over the albums, beta?' Neela's voice brought her back to earth.

After spending the better part of an hour flipping through the sepia-toned photographs with Neela on the surprisingly comfortable sofa, Satyadarshi bid her farewell, promising to update her when she solved Laxmi's murder. During her visit, she also scrutinized Mr Gandhar's phone, but as expected, it only included Laxmi's contact and no other information.

'May God bless you. Stay safe, Satyadarshi beta. It was nice having someone to talk to, you remind me of my daughter, Maya.' She pointed at a woman in one of the photographs, who looked nothing like the tall, slim, light-eyed Satyadarshi.

Satyadarshi took the phone from Neela's hand and entered her phone number into the contact list. 'Neela ji, I've saved my number on your phone. Anytime you feel lonely or just want to chat, call me.'

'Thank you, baccha.'

On the way home to Dadar from the Gandhars' apartment in Mahim, Satyadarshi boarded a local and leaned against the compartment door, watching the slums fly past. The juddering train was crowded, and the smell of sweat and wet dog persisted in the air, but being a local, Satyadarshi's olfactory senses were immune to it.

She made a mental note to call Neela Gandhar regularly, as she was worried about the newly bereaved, diminutive lady. Both her children lived in America and were visiting India for their father's funeral. Satyadarshi fretted over what would happen to Neela ji once they returned. *Maybe their mother can accompany them back.*

A reluctant smile made a cameo appearance on her lips when Twarita's voice piped up in her brain. 'You can't take care of everyone, SD. You can't be present everywhere. Learn to let go.'

I try, Twa. I really do. But old ladies are my Kryptonite. Besides food. And now, apparently, nerds with chin clefts.

When she disembarked from the train at the crowded platform, her thoughts returned to the case at hand. *Why did everyone in Laxmi's circle possess the same music textbook?*

She sidestepped the loud hawkers as she descended the Dadar East bridge. On crossing Bombay's famous fried snack outlet, Goli, the owner waved at her, his favourite customer, and beckoned her inside.

'Satyadarshi, I've just fried a fresh batch. And I promise you, this time no one will jumble your order with the spinach vada! Come on!' he said.

Her stomach grumbled, but good sense prevailed. 'Not today, Dada. Not even for the classic vada! Aai has made peas pulao.'

At his sympathetic glance, she shrugged. 'No option but to eat it.' She hailed a passing taxi. 'Hindu Colony, bhaiya.'

At times, family comes at the cost of cauterizing one's taste buds.

Midway through the ride, she changed her mind and asked the driver to take a detour, much to his grumbling protests. Hungry as she was, she needed time to think before facing home – before the unappetizing pulao was shoved down her gullet.

Shivaji Park was the ideal place to think. She didn't know anyone there and could walk uninterrupted, unlike at Hindu Colony, where someone or the other would accost her to repair their mobiles or fix their cable connections.

As Satyadarshi disembarked from the black-and-yellow taxi, she skirted across the colourful katta – the low, colourful boundary enclosing the rare open space in Mumbai, Shivaji Park. She purchased a cone of roasted peanuts from a woman hawker and traced a circle around the ground.

The setting golden disc kissed the sea's surface, rendering the sky ablaze in myriad colours, but Satyadarshi was blind to it – lost in her thoughts that danced and frolicked in her mind with abandon and no particular order. Music, mantras, murder and geriatric deaths ruled the roost.

And then, without warning, Jai.

Her case notes faded as visions of the hunky researcher sneaked in unannounced – his rumbling laughter, his brown-flecked eyes and his long, shapely fingers. His image flicked every other errant thought aside and reigned supreme.

She had met him once again since their first rendezvous, and by the end of the outing, she realized she wanted to meet him again. The only thing holding her back was the inevitable gloating expression on her mother's face.

And a lifetime of hearing, 'I told you so. Mother knows best.'

Still, thoughts of Jai persisted.

The man talks too much, Heart. But he is definitely eye candy. Why am I thinking of him?

And listen up, Heart. I don't do love anymore. You know what happened after the last prick who ditched me like a hot potato? It took me forever to feel again, to function and operate normally.

So, behave yourself.

We are not doing love.

10

Ragini's experiments in the kitchen had obviously failed, as a thick cloud of noxious-smelling smoke infiltrated the living room. Satyadarshi was glad that she had disabled the smoke detector ages ago, after numerous threats from their society and the fines levied upon them. Her heart sang at the thought that breakfast would be – thankfully – cancelled in their house today. At least, no home-cooked ones.

She walked into the still-smouldering kitchen and avoided her still-fuming mother's gaze as Ragini scrubbed a blackened pan, muttering under her breath. A few of the burnt pieces were visible on the mosaic-tiled kitchen floor, and Ragini crushed them underfoot as she moved about.

Without saying a word, Satyadarshi switched on the exhaust fan and moved to the living room, where she opened the windows to let the smoke out. Standing there, she looked out at the street, where the ever-present hawker was selling bananas on the pavement. She was tempted to get a dozen for them but didn't want to risk her mother's wrath.

She poured a bowl of honey-coated cornflakes and cold milk and exited the kitchen quickly. Quiet as a church mouse, she sat in a lotus position on the balcony, gazing at the verdant trees. Her personal slice of heaven. Balancing the bowl on her knee, she spooned the cereal into her mouth. Letting her mind wander aimlessly amid the birds' chirps and the sounds of people going about their usual routines. White noise always gave her brain space to stretch, to untangle whatever was troubling it.

To avoid her mother, who was still banging away at the pots and pans, Satyadarshi slipped into the music room. Even though she didn't sing or play as much as either she or Aai would have liked, being there felt like a warm embrace. Her eyes traced the framed portraits of M. S. Subbulakshmi, Bhimsen Joshi and Kishori Amonkar that graced the wall above a handmade veena-playing Goddess Saraswati idol – her Appa's handiwork. The space felt inviting, with several cushions of varied hues lying on the floor.

A heavy desk was wedged between two large, wood-framed windows with metal grills overlooking their tree-hugged street. This was Ajoba's domain – his favourite room. His black ergonomic chair looked forlorn, as if missing the man who used it. The surface of his work table was layered with dust, even though the rest of the place was spotless. Stacks of papers and that strange, stubborn junk people can't seem to part with sat atop it. Satyadarshi knew Aai wanted to clean the chamber but was procrastinating. Somehow, sorting through someone's leftover items sealed their absence. Made it more real ...

She shook her head to shake off the maudlin thoughts and looked at the windows. They were the best part of staying in an old apartment. Current Bombay houses didn't have wooden window frames. These extra-long ones, with their shutters, were from an era long gone. They were so tall, you could almost call them French windows – just a few inches short of the real thing.

Morning sunlight filtered in, soft and diffused, playing gentle peekaboo between the rustling branches. The room was dotted with musical paraphernalia: a half-open folder of yellowing notations, a brass lota they used for ritual riyaz – smudged with fingerprints – sat beside a chipped harmonium, ink-stained practice notebooks and a tabla pair capped with embroidered protectors. A koel's incessant calls accompanied the sound of the old, creaky fan spreading the humid air around the room.

Satyadarshi cocked her head as she heard the bird call out to its mate.

Koel, there is still sometime for the rains to hit. You have got the timings wrong, a month more before Bombay will be blessed by the rain gods.

She sat on a cotton dhurrie and scanned the room. Her eyes fell on Ajoba's tanpura, now used by Aai. Before it was his, it had belonged to Ajji – an inheritance, in a way.

She had been four when she first realized that even a tanpura had a gender. As a child, she often sneaked into the music room and ran her fingers over the many musical instruments there. Ajji's stringed one was her favourite. It was smooth as butter, coloured like melted jaggery. One day she hid there to do just that, only to find Dhrupad Mama had beaten her to it.

He was trying to coax a few notes out of her grandmother's stringed companion, but instead of gliding his finger along the daand, he was plucking the strings. Hearing her instrument's protests, Ajji had rushed in there and scolded her son.

'Dhrupad! This is a medium of my sadhana, my companion! Don't pluck it carelessly. You've shown no reverence for music, so why touch what belongs to me?'

Dhrupad snapped back, 'You allow Ragini to touch it, why not me?'

'Ragini understands its importance. Unlike you, she respects the tanpura. Anyway, as a girl, she is bound to pick it up and will follow in my footsteps. Like I followed my mother's.'

'Baba isn't a girl. Why do you let him touch it, then?' Her uncle sneered.

An emotion – one Satyadarshi later recognized as disgust – had crossed Ajji's face. 'Your Baba's view about our gharana, its traditions and his pedigree, give him more than enough reasons to use it, Dhrupad. Your attitude is one of disdain. You want to control music and not let it lead you towards salvation.'

She leaned in and took a deep breath. 'Sometimes I look at you and can smell the jealousy you fester in your heart.'

Her uncle's face darkened. 'Your genes didn't give me the talent to sing. How is that *my* fault?' he spluttered. After saying his piece, he had thrust the instrument into his mother's hands and stormed out, kicking a table on his way out.

Ajji noticed her granddaughter shivering in a corner and her face softened. In a rare loving gesture, she held out her arms. After a moment of hesitation, Satyadarshi had rushed into her grandmother's arms and inhaled her sandalwood and rose scent – something she could still catch in the air of the room at times.

Satyadarshi now picked up the mellow bronze gold tanpura and ran her fingers down its still smooth body – worn not by neglect, but by decades of loving use. Her index finger traced the hairline cracks, so similar to the laugh lines around Ajoba's mouth. A single faded red thread tied to the stem marked Ajji's passing. Her mother had tied it after Ajji's death. Her grandfather eschewed his instrument and started using Ajji's tanpura instead. He always said that in its notes, he heard her voice.

Whenever Aai finds it in herself to do it, she will tie another red thread in Ajoba's name.

As if touching the stringed tanpura had opened a portal, her grandmother – her guru's – voice floated in her head. 'Chakuli, this tanpura is not an instrument. It is the sky. You don't sing *with* it. You sing *into* it.'

'I'm losing my mind,' Satyadarshi said to the empty room and gently placed the instrument back in its place of honour.

Ragini had calmed down by the time Satyadarshi was ready to leave for work and even smiled at her.

When Satyadarshi threw her arms around Ragini, she patted her daughter's back. 'I'm sorry for burning breakfast, Darshi. I wanted to cook thalipeeth like Aai used to make. Paddu and I loved it, especially when she added homemade loni and thecha.'

She lowered her eyes. 'But while I put them on the griddle pan to cook, a solution to a composition in Raag Yaman sprung into my head.' Her eyebrows danced on her forehead. 'By the time I finished thinking, the thalipeeth was charred.'

'Not a problem, Aai. Let's try making it again this Sunday.'

'Yeah, Darshi. But what irked me the most was that the smoke made me forget the answer to my problem! Now I might have to burn something else to remember it.' Ragini joined Satyadarshi as they laughed.

Starting her car, Satyadarshi whooshed out the air she was holding in.

A lucky escape.

To her utmost delight, she reached Sion in under twenty minutes.

The day has already blessed me with two of the three lucky boons, what could be the third one?

Her phone's screen lit up, displaying her wallpaper. It was a picture of Satyadarshi and Baby Bimbette. She had stuck out her tongue and held her hands up like floppy bunny ears, while Baby Bimbette's lolling tongue and perky ears stole the show. Their photo always made her smile. But today, it did something else entirely – made her heart leap, spin and do a little fist-pump. A message from Jai.

Brain chipped in, *shush, Heart. No one asked you to beat so fast!*

❈

It's a good day when Bombay blesses you with moving traffic and an empty parking spot.

Satyadarshi let out a yodelling greeting to Twarita as she entered the office and stopped short.

Well, well, well. What do we have here?

Prateek leaned against the side of Twarita's desk while she sat in her chair. Satyadarshi's entry had cut Twarita off mid-chuckle, and she looked up, guilt written across her usually calm face.

As soon as he saw her, Prateek straightened and saluted her smartly. 'Good morning, madam.'

'Sub-Inspector Prateek! It's good to see you. And you don't need to salute me anymore. It's only for serving senior officers.'

'Why don't you join SD in her office while I type this report? Your incessant chatting will only disturb me,' said Twarita, waving them off.

Prateek followed Satyadarshi into her inner sanctum and waited until she was seated before pulling out a chair for himself.

'SD madam, whether you serve in the force or not, you

will always be my mentor. I've learnt so much while working under your command.'

'Ah, water under the bridge, Prateek. Anyway, what brings you here?'

'Well, I was visiting the Sion police station and after my conversation with Twarita yesterday, I thought I'd pop in to meet you.'

'I'm glad you did, Prateek,' smiled Satyadarshi.

'When Twarita called me to ask about the cases, I dug around. And while I can't show you the official files, I can give you a summary of what they contain.'

'Thank you. That means a lot to me.'

'Madam, what you've done for us – taught us in the course of an investigation – means the world to us. Whether it's Sub-Inspector Jatin, Constables Patil and Dhule or even Head Constable Trivedi, we're all firmly on your side. What the top brass did to you … should never have happened, but it hasn't dimmed your esteem in our eyes.'

'Thank you, Prateek. I had the best time working with you guys. Hope everyone's doing well in our chowki?'

'The more things change, the more they stay the same – just as you used to say, madam. Jatin is still hunting for a life partner, Patil is still dieting – crunching cucumber slices like a goat in meditation, Dhule is still playing referee for his grown-up kids and Trivedi is still an arsehole!' laughed Prateek.

'Status quo!' chuckled Satyadarshi. Returning to the case, she asked, 'So, what did the files contain?'

'Not surprisingly, almost nothing. Yesterday, I couldn't hand over Ms Madhyama's address to Twarita. So, here it is.' He slipped a chit to Satyadarshi, who noted down the address on her laptop.

'Once again, thanks, Prateek.'

'I looked at Ms Madhyama's file. The police have charged her cook with the murder. She'd had a fight with him over a wage-related issue, and he, in a fit of anger, murdered her.'

Satyadarshi cocked her head. 'Your tone implies you disagree, Prateek.'

'I'm not too happy with the investigation, madam. I think they found the first person who fit the bill and slapped the charges on him. But it's neither my jurisdiction nor my place to comment.'

'Noted. Anything in the Laxmi Pancham case?'

'Madam, I went through the evidence box at the Worli police naka. Their CCTV captured a figure, but the image is hazy. I can arrange for the recording. The murder was violent – as if the person had just let loose. Forensics found nothing that didn't belong to the room. No hair, no fingerprints. Even the murder weapon was missing. The murderer planned the entire event with no mistakes.'

'I've got access to the recordings from Mr Pancham. They're useless. We can barely make out the shape of the person, let alone the gender. The camera in her room was moved, and it couldn't capture much. I wonder if the murderer was aware of it or if it was just a lucky break.'

'The police don't seem to be interested in solving the

case. It has one foot in the cold-case grave and the other in apathy. You know how it goes, madam. The investigators feel it's a business rivalry case and are not too willing to spend the taxpayers' money on it.'

'I know. Did you, by any chance, get any information about the Priyam Gandhar case?'

'I checked in with the Mahim unit. The old man was bludgeoned to death, and in that part of the city, expecting CCTV is foolhardy. None of the neighbours heard anything, but then most of the building's residents are senior citizens. The watchman is the youngest amongst them and is sixty-three! The police even investigated his wife … '

'Neela? She wouldn't harm a fly! She'd probably end up feeding it,' interrupted Satyadarshi.

'Yes, madam. Nothing came of that. I also peeked into the Suhel Dhaivat file. We assume it was a Glock 22 pistol because the bullet was too fragmented for identification. As in the other cases, nothing was found at the scene. Do you think this could be a serial killer?'

'The victims are connected, Prateek. The killer changes methods each time, but they all knew each other. I don't know if it's one killer – or just coincidence. The clues take me nowhere. And everywhere.'

'But you always taught me there's no such thing as coincidence.'

'I could just be wrong, Prateek. This case has taught me that even my instincts can go haywire.'

11

Twarita came over to Satyadarshi's apartment on Saturday morning, their rare day off, just as her boss was trying – and failing – to wind herself out of the Gomukhasana.

In the end, it was Twarita who had to disentangle her. As thanks, Satyadarshi cooked kande pohe – Twarita's ultimate favourite, even more than Indori pohe. A preference her Indore-born mother considered grounds for disownment. But having been born in Maharashtra to a Marathi father, Twarita's palate was more inclined – and loyal – to her home state.

Indian moms and daughters – so much love in childhood, mild horror and distaste in the teens and an emotional stock market boom once the daughters hit their twenties. There has to be a graph for this. Jai must know. I'll ask him.

With Ragini out for the day, they had the apartment to themselves. While Satyadarshi rinsed the flattened rice and prepped the tempering, Twarita took charge of the coffee, beating it into a frothy, creamy swirl, like the expert she was.

'When did you start with yoga?' Twarita asked. 'If you'd

told me, we could've gone to the studio where I go every Sunday.'

'That is why!' Satyadarshi smirked. 'I started after visions of an unhealthy me, after Baby Bimbette's case. Made me realize how important exercise is.'

Once they were done, Twarita took one look at the dinner-plate-sized circles under her friend's eyes. 'You have been brooding too much, SD. And you're even more insufferable when you're brooding.' She raised her voice over Satyadarshi's vehement protests. 'You need to laugh. Or at least groan in despair at a terrible pun. So ... ' Twarita waved two pieces of paper at her, singing, ' ... I got us tickets.'

'No, Twa! Although I love you, your choice of movies sucks. To what? Don't tell me, it's the new Rohit Shetty film.' A mutinous expression settled over her features.

'Sheesh, no. Not his movie, but tickets to a play.'

'A play? Theatre wala? How is that *any* better?'

'Yes, a play that takes place in a theatre. You'll love it. It's fabulous.'

Satyadarshi narrowed her eyes. 'Not after the NCPA fiasco. And define fabulous.'

Twarita snorted. 'Hello? NCPA was all on you. No one asked you to scream out, "This is not how knives work!" in the middle of the act! Sheesh, I had to use all my charm to not get us banned.'

She winked at Satyadarshi. 'This one's different, SD. It's called *Inspector Rajnikant and the Case of the Missing Anda.* Full-too viral. I've heard it's a laugh riot.'

'Sounds like a felony against logic. *Inspector Rajnikant and the Case of the Missing Anda*? What is he, a hen?'

'No. He's a police officer, duh. And he's investigating a case where an egg is egg-napped. Which is exactly why you'll love it.'

'Umm, no. I'll hate every moment. You know how I despise police procedurals serials on TV.'

'Don't I know? You're always finding faults and muttering "Impossible" at every scene.'

'Because their plots and actions *are* impossible.'

'Well, you lost fair and square.'

'No … ' moaned Satyadarshi. 'Don't make this about our wager.' She glared. 'You promised not to weaponize my idiocy.'

Twarita just smiled as she dropped the tickets into Satyadarshi's bag.

❈

In the end, Satyadarshi had to go. It was a question of keeping a promise.

I hate it when I have to be all 'honour thy word'-y.

But she'd lost a movie trivia bet, so there was no chance of escape – or of Twarita forgetting.

Bombay had only two seasons: sweat and splash. In deference to the former, Satyadarshi picked a knee-length navy blue cotton dress with gathered pleats and slipped on her soft vegan leather pumps. Even a card-carrying nonconformist like her knew that showing up at Prithvi in crumpled pyjamas was a crime punishable by theatre crowd side-eyes.

She reached there with thirty minutes to spare and was killing time when her phone vibrated in her pocket. Yeah, dresses with pockets were a dream come true.

Twarita had bailed, with a message.

Last-minute emergency, SD. Flat tyre. Can't make it. But I want a review. Not a made-up one. YOU promised, and I want it.

So, rubbing her hands in glee and with an ear to her rumbling stomach, she decided to eat, skip the show and head home.

Bet be damned. If the 'better' can't make it, the 'bettee' is absolved.

She sat alone in a corner seat of the open-air cafe, sipping her cutting chai and bun maska, rolling her eyes at the milling hipsters. *If only eye-rolling were an Olympic event ...*

Satyadarshi spotted a tall, slim woman dressed in a fake fur coat making her entrance. The woman had paired it with gorgeous ankle boots that Satyadarshi instantly lusted after. She was in the middle of another eye-roll when someone tapped her on the shoulder. She turned – mid-bite, mid-eye-roll – and nearly choked.

Jai. In casual wear.

What was he doing here? Did Twarita plan this? No, she didn't know Jai. Or have his number.

'Didn't expect to see you here,' he said, grinning. Satyadarshi had only met him during working hours, either dressed in formal trousers or jeans, so Bermuda-clad Jai was ... interesting.

'Well, I'm not here by choice,' she sighed. 'I lost a dare and this is my punishment. But now Twa dumped me. I was counting on her to suffer through this disaster with me.' She shrugged. 'Misery needs company, especially when served with anda jokes. What are *you* doing here?'

'Tell me more about the bet, yeah?'

'Umm ... So, every Monday afternoon, to beat boredom, Twa and I have an impromptu quiz. She's a Bollywood addict, and this time, it was her chance to challenge me. Her question was the name of the movie in which Manoj Kumar's son lip-synced the song, "Neele Neele Ambar" on screen.'

'It's from *Kalaakaar*! That was Kunal Goswami, his son, I mean. It was a total 80s cheese fest,' grinned Jai.

'Sheesh, go away!' she groaned. 'Why didn't I remember that? I remembered "Neele Neele Ambar". I even remembered Kunal Goswami, or, as I called him, Kartik! But I called the movie *Love Story*. And Twarita pounced on me.'

'Tsk. Classic novice mistake,' Jai nodded solemnly.

'I hate you. You trivia-collecting person.'

Jai smirked and tapped the print on his The Doors T-shirt. 'Nerd, remember? To answer your question, I'm here because my office cubicle friend mentioned the bun maska at the Prithvi cafe was worth trying. And I'd heard a lot about the play too, so I thought two birds.' He eyed her plate, where two pieces of the famed bread lay oozing butter. 'Want to share one?'

'Get your own plate, mister!' she laughed as she scooted over, and he joined her at the table.

After they wolfed the food down, Jai convinced her to stay for the play, and she agreed, much to her own consternation. They gave away Twarita's ticket to the first guy they spotted in a pair of yellow printed shorts. When they entered the darkened theatre – Satyadarshi with trepidation and Jay with enthusiasm – the bell had just rung. It was about to start.

Just as she had expected, the play was ludicrous. Atrocious, even. The actors' accents were from nowhere on earth, and Inspector Rajnikant pronounced 'criminal' as 'creee-min-al'. *That was criminal in itself.*

And then came the murderer and kidnapper of the egg – Subramanian, the Pomeranian dog with an eye patch. Sigh.

As if dogs could kill, even Pomeranians.

Yeah, I can't understand why this play went viral. What's wrong with people?

But despite herself, Satyadarshi had found herself laughing at certain points. It was throat-tickling, nose-snorting, thigh-slapping kind of laughter, and poor Jai was often the victim of it. Rather, his thighs.

For once, I didn't roll my eyes or mutter 'impossible' out loud. I just ... let it be. I didn't think I'd laugh this much in Jai's company. Or feel this light.

And just like that, her brain whispered, *don't get too used to this.*

Once the hangover of the play wore off, Jai and Satyadarshi headed towards Juhu Beach – no discussion, just a quiet, mutual decision to extend the evening.

Their hands brushed now and then, distracting her far more than she'd admit.

Juhu was the only beach she tolerated – comparatively cleaner and not smelling like a mix of fish with body odour and halitosis in a closed room. *Well, it didn't stink that badly.*

By the time they reached, it was already crowded with people thronging the water. The circular moon was rising, and the hazy light cast ripples across the sea, highlighting the waves as they crashed into the sand.

The laughter from the play still lingered, but something between them had shifted. Like joy had evaporated, leaving behind a trace of acute awareness, a thread of the unknown. She glanced at Jai. He smiled. She smiled back, then immediately looked away.

'Hey, you okay?'

'Yeah,' she blurted. *Cool it, Darshi.*

Jai, sensing the moment needed a food miracle, dragged her towards a chaat stall. 'I've always wanted to try the famous Juhu pani puri. Want to join me?'

'When it comes to food, I'm always in!'

And just like that, the awkwardness popped like a puri.

Jai held two filled paper plates precariously, offering her one with mock ceremony. 'Your puri, my lady.'

Satyadarshi swallowed it, and the spicy water made her eyes water and nose run. 'This is just as I remembered.' As Jai raised his puri, she warned, 'Careful – it's spicy. Can you handle it?'

'Please, I'm from the land of mirchi thecha!'

'Dude, Pune is famous for its sweet chaats, not the spicy ones!'

He narrowed his eyes as he put the ball in and spoke around it. 'Watch me and cry!'

She shrugged, wiping her mouth and smiled in increasing amusement as Jai's nose turned red and tears streamed down his cheeks.

'Haha. Look who's crying, wimp!' she teased.

'That was … unexpected! Back home, the chaat isn't this fiery. My mouth might be on fire, but damn, it was good.'

She rummaged through her bag and took out the bottle she always carried, handing it over to him. 'Here, fire-dragon, knock yourself out.'

They walked along the surf, shoes in hand, waves licking their toes.

'Why do you think Twarita ditched you?' he asked, kicking a seashell.

'Not sure if she ditched me, per se. She probably sensed I needed this more than she did. The case I'm on … it's heavy.'

'Twarita is a smart woman.'

'The smartest. The sweetest. I don't know what I'd do without her.'

'Even though she made you watch the Subramanian peeing on stage?'

She shuddered. 'That was such a travesty. But yes, even then.'

On the way home, she wished she could pause this

moment – case and chaos be damned – for a while longer. The break, though forced, had recharged her.

But tomorrow, she was headed to Dombivli.

Even a one-eyed Subramanian was preferable to *that*.

He didn't chant today. Today was a day for something different.

And today, he craved silence.

Silence let him concentrate, to absorb knowledge.

Over time, the thrill of using another's space became an addiction. Flats between tenants were always safer. He had long ago learnt that brokers were the real gatekeepers of the city and how to slip through their cracks. An empty flat promised silence without interruption, if one was patient enough. He would wait and watch, noting which windows stayed dark for weeks, which door frames lost their nameplates, which corridors gathered dust.

The current flat – one where he had broken into just for kicks – was bare, stripped to bone. Not even a water bottle left behind.

On the cold floor lay an open medical textbook, its pages illuminated by the yellow light of the overhead bulb. He had brought it along and had been fixated for hours on the same page: *Chapter 14: Manual Strangulation and the Fracture of the Hyoid Bone.*

He didn't read it the way people read. He studied it as a musician studies notation. Like a killer, methodical.

His eyes lingered on the diagram of the hyoid – a fragile, floating bone shaped like a horseshoe.

Reading aloud, he said. 'The hyoid breaks with a soft pop.'

He smiled.

'Common in strangulations involving disproportionate force or ritualistic grip.'

Disproportionate force. Ritualistic grip.

He underlined the words with calm precision. The lines were straight, almost as if drawn with a ruler.

Next to the book lay his own notes – inked with care, sketched lines, measurements, pressure ranges:

2 thumbs – 3 seconds – vocal cords collapse.

5 seconds – hypoxia-induced disorientation.

10–12 seconds – loss of consciousness.

27 seconds – God enters.

He liked that last line. It made the science seem almost poetic.

The skin of his palms stretched tight as he flexed his grip and curled them around an imaginary neck. His thumbs would position themselves right over her vocal cords. All he had to do was hold the pressure for twenty-seven seconds. Not even half a minute.

He practised again, timing himself against the second hand of his black Titan watch, his trusted metronome, his breath steady. His fingers stayed curled, holding the right posture. He tried it a few times, satisfied with how calm his hands were. How undisturbed his heart remained.

He picked up the book and sniffed it. He loved them. He could part with anything, but never with them – whatever happened. They were his inheritance. His doctrine.

On a new sheet, he wrote: 'Control is not violence. It's a kind of music. The body is an instrument. You must know where it bends ... and where it breaks. And how you can break it.'

Rising, he collected his stuff and switched off the bulb. The darkness greeted him like an old friend. Outside, a dog howled. Then, there was a quivering silence.

Inside, only breath remained.

The kind of breath that came before the first note of a raga – or the last breath of someone who never saw it coming.

12

Potholes. People. Poli Bhaji Kendras. The three 'P's that define Dombivli.

Designed like a rabbit's warren, the barely there lanes criss-crossed the city, mirroring the live electric wires that hung above like levitating snakes in the skies. There was a vibe in this central suburb – an incessant, unending white noise of local cuss words, the varying pitches of hawkers and a playlist comprising several owls' loopy psychotic songs alternating with nails on a blackboard. Satyadarshi's shapely ears threatened to dislodge themselves in protest against the decibels.

The auto driver plucked dirt from his nails, using his overgrown pinky nail as leverage, while the vehicle stood in an unscheduled, unwarranted jam at the mouth of a narrow lane. The entry was crammed with motorcycles, autos and Maruti Altos, all waiting for the traffic jam to clear.

She craned her neck to see what the fuss was about. A wedding procession, blissfully unconcerned about the traffic pile-up, was making its painstakingly slow pilgrimage across the street. People danced with abandon and even used the potholes as impromptu dance pits!

Satyadarshi's jaw dropped to the floor as she watched the chaos unfold.

'How far to Garibacha Wada?'

The auto driver paused, picked his nose and turned towards her. 'Madam ji, the moment the jam frees up, we'll reach in seven minutes. It's not very far from here.'

She glared at the congested lane ahead, wondering if walking would have been a better option.

⁂

One hour later, Satyadarshi – now armed with a more colourful vocabulary and a broader library of shady film songs – disembarked from the rickshaw.

In front of her stood a house tiled to perfection. Glossy beige and brown tiles covered every inch of the facade, extending even to the Tulsi Vrindavan on the veranda. The holy basil plant appeared worse for wear – its dried, shrivelled leaves clinging to the stem in search of better times.

Satyadarshi pulled out her ever-present water bottle from her bag and poured some into the plant.

Grow well, little plant.

Before ascending the four steps, she scanned the garden that once must have thrived. It was apparent that since Ms Madhyama's death, it too had been dying – one plant at a time. The trellis that had once supported the tomato plant

– the murder weapon – was missing. The tomatoes, plump and crimson, looked oddly alive in a space now tinged with decay.

Shaking her head, she rang the bell. She was immediately inundated by a screechy version of 'Om Jai Jagadish Hare'. She clamped her hands over her ears as a woman opened the door.

'We aren't buying anything,' she said, about to slam the door shut.

'Wait, Purva! I'm Satyadarshi. We spoke on the phone yesterday. Sorry I'm late. I got stuck in traffic.'

'Let me guess. A wedding procession?' Purva opened the door wide and waved her inside.

'Yes! How did you guess?' Satyadarshi asked.

'I stayed in Dombivli for ages before getting married. Trust me, you're experiencing a very subdued version of what life used to be. Come on in.'

Purva led Satyadarshi through a passage that opened into an empty hall. The inner walls were covered with ... tiles. The same pattern adorned both the walls and the floor.

Diwali cleaning must be a quick affair. A swipe here, a swipe there, and you're done.

Thankfully, the ceiling was free of ceramic tiles. The POP structure displayed more LEDs than the combined sparkle of the Andromeda and the Milky Way, set against the deep, blood-red paint. In the rectangular room, it cast a faint crimson glow. The lack of proper ventilation and natural light added to the intensity of the hue.

Well, at least, the cockroach colonies will be fewer. They hate red light. Small mercies.

The rest of the walls were egg white. The room lacked furniture or furnishing, save for three chairs placed haphazardly.

'I'm so sorry about your mother, Purva,' said Satyadarshi, placing a hand on her arm as they sat.

Purva closed her eyes briefly. 'Thank you. It's been difficult. Especially since someone killed Ma while she was tending her garden. After Daddy's death, she'd taken to gardening with all the gusto of a woman trying to fill a hole in her life. She planted everything – vegetables, herbs and even fruits! Our neighbours depended on her for their fresh veggies supply.' A wistful smile softened her face, the kind that blooms when memory and grief walk hand in hand.

'Has the police been able to identify a person of interest?'

'Yes, they've held her cook responsible. Apparently, he and Ma argued over the declining quality of the food he cooked. And in a fit of rage, he throttled her with the first thing he could lay his hands on – a wire.' Purva shook her head.

'You don't believe their version?'

'No, but who cares? Ramu Kaka was a frail sixty-five-year-old man suffering from arthritis. How could he have cut a stray wire from the trellis? He didn't have the strength to strangle Ma. They were great friends – and what was his motive? I think the police just wanted the case closed and Ramu Kaka checked all their boxes.'

Tears flowed down Purva's cheeks. 'In the end, it doesn't get Ma back, does it?'

Satyadarshi nodded.

'Anyway, we've got to keep moving on. Over the phone, you mentioned that you were investigating a case, and that it brought you to Ma's door,' Purva said, making a visible effort to control her tears.

'Yes. Your mother was friends with Ms Laxmi Pancham, and they spoke fairly often over the phone. Would you know anything about it?'

'No, Satyadarshi. My elder sister, Shaila, was closer to Ma and knew her day-to-day activities. She lives in Kalyan; it's just a hop, skip and jump away. She was in the US when Ma was ... I can't even say it.' She sighed and tried again. 'When someone murdered Ma. Shaila's son was undergoing treatment there for a rare disease. He's recovered now and Shaila will be returning tomorrow. That's why I've been handling everything in her absence.

'Shaila didi doesn't even know I've cleared out Ma's house. All the rubbish has been sold off to the raddiwallah. She had so many books and papers! I donated her old clothes and the worn-out furniture has been discarded.'

As soon as she heard those words, a shadow fell across Satyadarshi's face.

Was coming here a waste of my time? So much for clues. So much for preservation. A wire trellis – gone. A book likely sold for twelve rupees a kilo.

Dombivli, 1. Darshi, 0.

13

A dingy and grimy shop, where even the paint had stopped watching itself peel, stood sandwiched between a barber and a dhobi shop. A signpost – probably rescued from raddi itself and modified – hung over it. 'New Bhavani Old Paper Mart' was scribbled across it.

An infant, dressed in nothing but a thin silver chain with tiny bells around its waist, crawled and chewed a rattle, trapped inside a fort of empty Bisleri five-litre cans and plastic oil cans.

Grease marks dominated the shop's walls, and everything was haphazardly placed in uneven piles, tottering on the brink of toppling over if one breathed too hard in their direction. Satyadarshi brushed aside the comics strung along a string as she stepped inside the shop. She was pleased to note some familiar ones – *Champak, Chacha Chaudhary, Chitralekha.*

'Bhaiya, do you have this book?' she asked, holding up her almost-famous book on music.

The bald, pot-bellied man scratched his crotch through his grey lungi as he crossed his legs. Apart from his head, his entire body was covered with hair. Tufts of it shot out of his large ears, accentuating them. He wore a stained vest that strained to cover his vast stomach. He shook his pockmarked face, his eyes not even bothering to settle on the book Satyadarshi held. 'I don't know. You can look around, and if you find it, you can buy it for two hundred rupees.'

Cursing her luck, Satyadarshi gazed around the unkempt, untidy 3x6 shop, crammed with rejects from everyone's households. Glass jars, newspapers turning yellow, files, mutilated toys, dented vessels and broken pots filled every inch of the place. One sagging shelf contained only papers and notebooks. A tower of metallic boxes stood blocking it.

'Purva sold you a few things from Ms Madhyama's house in Garibacha Wada, right? Where have you kept them?' she asked.

For her efforts, she was given a blank stare and a hairy shoulder shrug. Satyadarshi started to search the shop but barely had the luxury of moving around. There was no sign of the book anywhere in the crowded landfill. She moved towards the shelf but had to shift the cans before reaching it.

'Can you help me move the dabbas to the other side?' she asked. *It's like talking to a wall.*

The man, continuing to stare into space, remained immobile.

Sighing loudly, Satyadarshi painstakingly picked up each metallic carton and placed it on the ground, forming stacks of five each. They were dirty and oily and stained her peach Lucknowi kurti.

Ma is going to scream when she sees the state of my clothes.

Once she cleared the obstructions, she rummaged through each paper pile and sifted through them. Not finding it amongst the pile, she began the reverse process of restacking the cans atop each other, or else there would be no place to even move.

The only spot left in the coffin-disguised-as-a-shop was an orange-coloured oil can that had been cut to act as a dustbin. Taking a deep breath to fortify her resolve, Satyadarshi dug in. Amongst the peanut shells, orange peels and some unknown debris she refused to dwell on, she found a page that belonged to the book.

Triumphant, she stood up and, in her haste, knocked the can over. Trapped beneath its oily bottom was the book she sought – rundown, torn and stained. She quickly turned it over, and miraculously, the last page had survived the onslaught. The Garuda Mantra greeted her like a sly old friend.

She cradled the slim book like a wounded bird – forgotten, filthy, but still breathing. Still speaking.

'I'll pay you ten rupees for this book,' she bargained.

'Fifty,' he countered.

'Twenty.'

'Deal.'

Smiling like a cat that had swallowed the canary, Satyadarshi stepped out of the shop ...

And promptly crashed into a dysfunctional walker from hell. *Damn.*

The mustard oil lamp on the yellow cloth spread its light and pungent odour in the small room. To the man who sat cross-legged, the brightness of the lamp didn't matter. Nor did its aroma.

The man was lost in chanting the Baglamukhi Maran Mantra. He was on his 3599th incantation. His hoarse voice stayed on the beat, reciting the Beej Mantra in the same intonation.

Om Hreem Baglamukhi /
Sarvdushtanaam Vacham Mukham Padam /
Stambhay Jeevham Keelay Buddhim /
Vinashaya Hreem Om Svaha ||

As the last recitation rolled off his tongue, his eyes sprang open, staring at the oil wick. *Six down, seven more days to go. Victory is within my grasp.*

He placed the rosary on the raised platform and used the yellow cloth around his neck to swab his sweaty forehead, leaving streaks of turmeric on his face. Everything was yellow in the room, and the colour reflected in his eyes, making them appear jaundiced.

The thirteen-day gruelling ritual should have begun last month, but a sudden work trip had derailed his plans. Now that he was back, he initiated it. Once it started, it was not to be stopped under any circumstances. And he would ensure he went through it.

His enemies had to be defeated. The girl was nipping at his heels, and this was the only way to keep her at bay. Ma Baglamukhi protected her followers and fulfilled all their wishes. And his wishes were so simple – annihilation of his enemies. Now, enemy.

He gazed at his black Titan watch – the only concession to another colour in the room. Time had crossed into the 3:00 a.m. threshold. He closed his eyes, and a burst of laughter rumbled out, birthing in his stomach.

Two days to go.

The treasure would be his – in every sense of the word. The temple may be ruled by the royals, but he was going to prove that he had the bluest blood amongst them.

He would be the penultimate guru.

Swaha.

14

A strange unease clung to Satyadarshi's skin that morning, like cobwebs she couldn't shake off. She dismissed it, blaming the weather, which was high on humidity and zero on rain, but heavy with grey cloud cover. She needed her adrak chai before facing the world outside and made her way to the kitchen.

At the threshold, she paused. Ragini was singing – a voice like an angel's – while cooking what was most likely a torturous, tasteless nachni cheela for breakfast. Savouring the song, she sat at the table, reading the paper, when her phone buzzed. It was a message from Jai.

Have you ever had food at Pancham?

A fleeting smile migrated across her lips as she responded.

Do fish have gills?

His reply was immediate.

Every fish except dolphins. They breathe via a blowhole. Anyway, yesterday the office folks were talking about Pancham.

Satyadarshi tapped her index finger on her lips as she mentally reviewed her roster.

This is interesting. I'm meeting my frustrated accountant in the Fort area this afternoon. Want to have an early lunch at Pancham Puriwale?

Her phone pinged again, a musical symphony.

Done, but my treat.

Her fingers flew over the keypad.

Dutch. And it's final.

Jai responded with Deal.

Another quick message from him puzzled her for a minute before she chuckled.

Whales don't have gills either.

Oh, lord. Geeky.

Since their initial meeting, Jai and Satyadarshi had continued their nascent friendship – if she could really call it that – and chatted on and off until it became a daily ritual. Jai often sought her advice about different restaurants or train routes.

His office was near Nariman Point, and whenever she happened to be in that part of town, they met for a quick meal or coffee, if their schedules allowed. He had maintained his nerdy status but was starting to grow on Satyadarshi. They had similar tastes in books and music, and despite his athletic physique, Jai – like her – was a foodie. She made a mental note to ask him if he practised yoga. Twarita had finally roped her into the Sunday yoga class, and now, every morning at 7:00 a.m., they were stretching and contorting. And then demolishing pav bhaji at Shiv Sagar.

Satyadarshi had recently discovered – after a whole lot of cajoling to share his work – Jai was an annoyingly good writer. His stories ranged from thoughtful ones to sheer laugh riots. Satire ran in his blood, a trait she understood well. Except, in her case, it was sarcasm.

By mutual yet unspoken consent, they had decided to keep their meetings a secret from their respective nosy mothers. They didn't want the mothers to have the satisfaction. Satyadarshi had even stored Jai's number in her cell phone as Jaya. *Take that, Aai!*

Thinking about the messages, she wondered where her father was as he hadn't messaged her incessantly for a couple of days. Then she remembered Appa was out of town for an academic conference in Lonavla. *I'll meet him for our now-regular lunch when he returns.*

Satyadarshi hummed a song as she continued reading the newspaper. Ragini observed her from the kitchen while flipping the pancake. The gamut of expressions crossing Satyadarshi's face wasn't lost on her, and she was convinced the messages were from Jai. She bit her lip to supress a smile as she smeared the nachni batter on the hot tawa, and made a mental note to message Vaiju – her friend and Jai's mother – after she finished her music classes.

We'll gloat together. The kids thought their mothers were clueless – had no idea how perfectly they fit. Haha. 'Darshi, I've got to meet my friend after the Gandharva examination, so today's dinner is your headache. I'll eat before I get home. Don't eat junk food,' warned Ragini as she placed the piping hot cheela on Satyadarshi's plate.

'Whom are you meeting?' Satyadarshi made a face at her plate as she spread tomato ketchup over it.

'My college friends. We haven't met in ages. We're planning to watch a movie after an early dinner.'

Satyadarshi hesitantly bit into the cheela. 'This isn't that bad, Aai. Maybe there's some hope for you when it comes to cooking. I thought Fridays were for the Babulnath temple.'

'Darshi! Monday is Lord Shiva's day, not Friday. When will you remember these details? How many times have I told you?'

'I thought all days belonged to the gods,' parried Satyadarshi.

'Don't be impudent, child!'

'How am I being impudent? You never miss visiting the Babulnath temple every first Monday of each month, do you?'

'Never have I missed it. There's so much peace in that temple.'

'How come you never take me with you?'

'Taking you with me will defeat the purpose, Darshi. You'll crib and criticize everything. *Why are people not picking up the flowers they dropped? Why do we have to give dakshina?* Like your father, you have no patience for anything remotely religious. I'd rather go alone than take you!' Ragini huffed, then took a breath and continued with a twinkle in her eye, 'Forget about that, any special plans for today?'

'Special plans? Nope. Nothing. I've got to visit my company accountant to sign a few documents for tax stuff. So, I'll be going by train to the office.'

'Oh, town area. That's where Jai works, right? You can meet him too – if he's free, of course.'

'Does he?' She raised one shoulder. 'Why should I meet him, Aai? Are you still carrying on with your matchmaking nonsense?'

'Shoo. Not at all. Such a useless child you are, Darshi! Now, do you want more of this healthy pancake?'

⁂

Jai was waiting outside the deceptively simple Pancham Puriwale restaurant when Satyadarshi arrived. He was leaning against the wall, scanning every person who walked in. With his sunglasses on, he was difficult to recognize.

'Hey! You're looking good, Satyadarshi!' He exclaimed as he spotted her.

She smiled and gestured for him to enter the restaurant so he wouldn't see the redness growing in her cheeks. Resting against the cool steel perforated seats was a pleasure after the unrelenting heat outside. Jai perused the menu and placed it down with a sigh.

'What's good here?' he asked. 'I can't make up my mind and I'm open to suggestions. You know your food. Help me out, please.'

'Music to my ears.' Flashing a cheeky grin, Satyadarshi

turned towards the server. 'Bhaiya, two masala puris with chane ki sabji. And four glasses of masala chaas with extra coriander leaves.' She turned to Jai as he left with the order.

'You're going to love the food here.'

'I'm sure I will. I've heard a lot about this place. It's older than CST and has still maintained its quality. That in itself is impressive. But tell me, why four buttermilk glasses?'

'Oh, only one's for you, dude. The other three are mine! Buttermilk runs in my veins – besides tea, coffee and kala khatta soda. Yeah, Pancham is quite iconic. And it fits in right with your PhD on ancient stuff. How's that going, by the way?'

'Oh, yes. I stumbled upon a treasure trove the other day – a rare white paper on the seven folks who formed Ashoka's Unknown Seven. The paper made an interesting correlation. This may interest you since you come from a musical background, Satyadarshi.'

This time, instead of getting annoyed, she smiled at him.

'The paper opines that to hide the septet in plain sight, Ashoka contacted the musicians and entrusted them with the responsibility of understanding and expanding their knowledge in different streams besides music. The author makes an educated guess that the seven swars – Sa Re Ga Ma Pa Dha and Ni – may conceal more than just their musical notes. Neat, right?'

'Yeah. So why musicians?' Satyadarshi asked, struggling to concentrate as the aroma of freshly fried puris invaded her senses.

'He felt musicians wouldn't need a reason to meet and the septet could visit each other freely without raising suspicions. It was quite a smart thing to do.'

'Who was the paper's author?'

'Dr Dhrupad Ni ... '

'I should've guessed it! He's my maternal uncle,' Satyadarshi cut in. 'Dhrupad Mama. Yup, that's him. He works with the Architectural Society of India. Mama spearheaded the Vishnu temple project. He was the guy who led his team to open the secret chambers in the temple. He practically founded the dork academy. You guys would fit perfectly well.' She pointed at the salt and pepper shakers shaped like two figurines locked in a tight embrace. 'Like them!'

His eyes grew big. 'Wait – Dhrupad Sir is *your* mama? I've read his paper on sonic harmonics in temple chambers ... twice. Okay, three times. He's kind of a big deal in nerdy history circles.'

'He's a big deal in pain-in-the-neck circles, too,' she snorted.

'Wow! He's something else! Do you think you can introduce me to him?' He grinned, ignoring the dig. And her heart puffed up like a puri.

'Yeah, I will. But he's – how do I put this delicately – weird? Too darned knowledgeable and unable to adjust to the stupidity and mediocrity surrounding him. So don't take offence if he ignores you. We're quite used to his behaviour. He and Aai are always fighting over trivial issues. Don't say I didn't warn you.'

'Are you calling me stupid?' Jai said in mock anger. He placed his hand over his heart. 'Or even worse, mediocre?'

'Stay calm and eat Pancham puris!' laughed Satyadarshi as the server placed two plates with a heavenly aroma along with four glasses of chilled chaas in front of them, pushing the salt and pepper shakers aside.

After playfully arguing over the bill and splitting it half-and-half, Jai teased her about her three buttermilk glasses as they strolled towards a paan shop, arguing over which one was the best.

However, instead of opting for the betel leaf offering, they picked up ten pink Pan Pasand candies.

A gentle breeze twirled her purple dress around her knees. Against her better judgement, Satyadarshi had dressed with care that day, tying her hair into a high ponytail and slipping on her favourite bullet earrings, their dangling charm accentuating her long neck. She felt a bit embarrassed about the outfit, not wanting to send Jai the wrong signal, yet secretly hoping he would misread it anyway.

Jai, as always, sported formal trousers, an executive blue shirt and sleek black loafers. He looked good enough to eat.

Satyadarshi popped the hard-boiled candy into her mouth and spoke as she savoured it. 'While I do like this candy, I think we should have stuck to the paan. What thinks you?'

'Why?'

'It always irritates the roof of my mouth, and I end up carrying three for Twa – it's our little unspoken pact.'

'You talk about her with such warmth; you two must be close. Close enough for her to force you into watching *Inspector Rajnikant and the Case of the Missing Anda,*' Jai observed.

Crunch. The sweet splintered in her mouth. 'I have suppressed that memory, so I have no idea of what you're speaking of,' she said, brushing the sugary bits from her tongue. 'Yes, Twa and I were friends from the time I was a serving police officer. I was the officer who filed an FIR against her husband for domestic violence, and … we clicked. Our friendship grew from that day onwards, and when I left the police, she needed a job and I, a manager. So, it worked out. And as they say, the rest is history.' Her eyes sparkled as she wagged a warning finger at him. 'Not a word, Jai!'

His laughter bubbled up, prompting her to add, 'Sometimes I think you've been a victim of those hypnotism tricks – say a word and you act?' She gave his arm a playful nudge. 'Your trigger word is "history". Uff, your "what-happened" obsession is next-level!'

Still chuckling, he slid his arm around her shoulder, his body pressing close, his candy-sweet breath warm against her cheek. A shiver raced up her spine, settling near her heart, quickening her pulse. 'I promise, madam. No more sentences with historical references will escape my lips!'

At 'lips,' her eyes traced his inviting, luscious mouth, time slipping away from her. She jolted back when she realized he had stopped speaking, his intense eyes holding hers. He tucked a stray lock behind her ear, his lips brushing the top edge, sending a tremor through her. 'Satyadarshi ... '

Before he could finish, a loud bark erupted at her feet, startling them. A pug circled her, yapping with joy.

'Baby Bimbette?' she whispered, still caught in the moment, still pressed very close to Jai. The dog woofed, wagging his curly tail. She finally managed to take a step back and knelt to check on him.

'Baby Bimbette?' Jai snorted.

'Shush! I'll tell you the story later. What are you doing here?' She turned to Jai. 'He's from Colaba!'

The dog's rainbow-coloured leash trailed behind him like a veil, and he was panting heavily. Her heart sank as she noticed how much weight Baby Bimbette had lost. His beady eyes were almost popping out of his gaunt face, and his body now resembled a flute rather than an accordion.

'Aww, I missed you so much, Baby Bimbette!' She peppered tiny kisses on his nose. 'What happened to you, baccha?' she cooed, stroking his massive head as he nuzzled her arm.

'Do you know this little guy?' Baby Bimbette turned his attention to Jai and contorted his short body to reach across and lick him on his neck, making him chuckle.

Oh, so Jai is ticklish!

'I didn't know you liked dogs, Jai!' she said.

For the second time, his reply was cut off by a squeal – this time, the human kind. Preia limped up to where they stood, breathing hard. Gone were the classy sarees and jumpsuits. She was dressed in faded pyjamas and a cream tee, looking unglamorous next to Satyadarshi. Which did not happen very often. Or at all.

'Oh my gosh, Satyadarshi! You found my poochie-poo! I thought I'd lost him forever. He escaped and ran away, and I've been chasing him.' She gestured to her blood-red stilettos, one shorter than the other. 'The brand duped me! One jog and the heel snapped like a breadstick.'

Satyadarshi's and Jai's eyes met, sharing a silent thought: *who wears heels to walk their dog?*

'I need your help again, Satyadarshi,' pleaded Preia.

15

Excusing herself – leaving Preia to catch her breath and Jai to cuddle with Baby Bimbette, who was snug in his arms – Satyadarshi called to cancel her appointment with her chartered accountant. After Mr Pancham's cheque had cleared, her bank balance was plumper than poor Baby Bimbette, and the tax man could courier the documents to her office, anyway.

When she returned to the trio, Jai suggested, 'Ladies and gentleman, let's cab it up to Marine Drive – Baby Bimbette needs a breather, and Preia also has a story to tell us. My office is quite close, so I can leave for my 3:00 p.m. meeting.'

Her heart fluttered at Jai's thoughtfulness. They hailed a taxi; the cabbie kept throwing dubious looks at Baby Bimbette, who was nestled between Satyadarshi and Jai, licking their knees in turns while Preia rode shotgun.

On the seafront, they stopped at Geoffrey's. Preia knew the owners, who graciously permitted her dog inside. After placing their drink order – cold coffee for Satyadarshi, a ginger ale for Jai, a Manhattan for Preia, and of course, iced water for the pug – Preia began.

'Have you noticed how much weight Baby Bimbette has lost?' At his name, his ears perked, and he licked Satyadarshi's feet, his icy tongue startling her. 'He's as thin as a vaping stick!'

'Yes. I figured it was the diet regime you'd started him on.'

Jai's eyebrows arched at Satyadarshi's comment and she mouthed 'later' to him.

'Yes, initially he resisted, but eventually he adjusted and his weight returned to normal. But lately, he's lost all interest in eating and seems distracted. He's so listless! Even the new stuff from our sponsors doesn't get a rise out of him, including the squeaky chicken he used to love.' Preia took a large gulp of her drink. 'The companies are threatening to jump ship. Again. They complain that your doggy is too thin and uninterested in any toys or treats. I can't keep losing money like this, Satyadarshi!'

'Have you taken him to the vet?' asked Jai.

'Oh, yes,' said Preia, twisting her long tresses into a loose bun on top of her head. 'He said it could be because Baby has smelt a dog in heat near our flat. I then asked Charan … '

Satyadarshi cut in to give Jai some context, 'His walker.'

'Yes, his walker,' continued Preia. 'Charan took him past a new construction site near Shalaka, where we live, and there he met a … ' Her pert nose scrunched in utter disgust. ' … a mangy female dog, and she's ensnared him in her net. The bitch has bewitched him! I think she dreams of moving up in life and wants to hitch her wagon to my Baby Bimbette.'

She huffed and signalled for another drink, her face set with resolve. 'But I won't let her schemes succeed!'

Twarita's laughter echoed in Satyadarshi's mind, and she bit her lip to stifle her grin. She nearly lost it when she caught Jai's half-smile lingering there, but managed to rein it in. 'Preia, how can I assist you?'

'Satyadarshi, I have unshakable faith in you! You worked miracles last time, figuring out why my doggy was getting so plump – I nearly bought a new fridge with a biometric lock, but you saved me lakhs with your solution! Now, I'm pleading again: free Baby Bimbette from this unholy infatuation!'

Jai glanced at his watch, a brown leather-strapped Tommy Hilfiger, and gestured for the cheque. Preia waved him off. 'No need, my sponsors cover it. Drinks are on the house.'

'Oh, okay. I must dash – very boring meetings await. Satyadarshi, I'll message you,' Jai said, squeezing her hand. Turning to Preia, he added, 'Lovely meeting you and Baby Bimbette. Best of luck!'

Satyadarshi struggled to hide her disappointment as he left. 'Preia, I'm not sure what I can do here … '

'I want you to find the vixen and get her to release my boy from her evil clutches.'

'You do realize these are dogs we're dealing with, right? I can't make them *do* anything! Except maybe shake hands,' Satyadarshi protested.

'That is your problem. I'm sending the money across to your account – same amount, and I want the same pronto results!' Saying that, Preia rose, waved to the owner, gathered her stuff and walked out with Baby Bimbette in tow, with as much as grace as a person wearing a single heel could manage.

Satyadarshi lay her head on the table, gently tapping it.

How do I sway a dog's heart? God, save me.

Feeling uneasy about not covering the drinks, she approached the cash counter and addressed the owner.

'Hey, I'm Satyadarshi. How do I settle the bill for the drinks we just had?'

'Oh, not a problem. Preia brings plenty of business for us. Are you also an influencer like her?'

'Oh, no, I run a detective agency.'

'Why not leave your card with me? If anyone needs a private dick, I'll point them your way!' he chuckled.

With a mock salute, she handed over a few of her cards and stepped into the blazing sun, sliding on her sunglasses.

So, being a woman, am I still a 'private dick'? 'Private ovary'? Ugh, no. Maybe 'private dame' has a ring to it – less cringe, at least.

Satyadarshi dialled Twarita, yanking the phone from her ear as her assistant-cum-mischief-maker erupted in laughter and squeals of delight.

'What are you going to do, SD? What's the next move?' She asked once she caught her breath.

'Step one is calling Charan to figure out the exact location of Ms LoverGirl. After that, I am stumped! Any suggestions?'

'None whatsoever. But may I make a request?'

'Yeah?'

'Please record your chat with Ms LoverGirl's human? I need the entertainment!'

Grinning, Satyadarshi hung up mid-Twarita's maniacal cackle, savouring the silence. She scrolled through her contacts and hit Charan's number. The man, as always, never wasted time on pleasantries. Two rings later, he rattled off the address, complete with directions only a local would find normal. 'Landmark? Just ask for Shyamlal's sugarcane stall near the third paanwallah. Not the first two, madam. Those fellows are frauds.'

She pinched the bridge of her nose, suppressing a smile. Typical – but enough.

Having pinpointed Pari's regular haunts, Satyadarshi debated whether she should walk or take a taxi. She missed her Alto and wished she had driven into town. Picking up a chilled, ginger-rich sugarcane juice from the third guy – minus the ice – she set off on foot to the place where the current bane of her existence resided.

The construction site mirrored every other chaotic spot she'd encountered: mayhem, noise and a swarm of workers. A peculiar smell lingered there – women cooking over open fires, kids playing nearby.

Charan had only shared the dog's name with her, not her human's. She strode towards the workers' living quarters, where tents lay cobbled together from colourful patchwork sheets. A few women gossiped beneath a makeshift shelter. The late afternoon sun exacted its revenge, cranking up the humidity and heat. Satyadarshi wiped her upper lip and muttered under her breath. *Should have taken a desk job. But no, madam wanted to save the world. And look where it's got me? Negotiating with dogs about their love lives. Bollywood could adapt my life into a movie.*

A fresh wave of absurdism washed over. *But money was money and bills needed to be paid.* She approached the women, speaking to one of them in Hindi.

'Does a dog named Pari stay here?'

'Yes,' one woman replied. 'Why do you want to know?'

'I ... erm ... wanted to meet her,' Satyadarshi finished lamely, earning a pitying glance before the woman returned to her chat but pointed her in the right direction.

Feeling like the world's biggest fool, yet fuelled by her love for Baby Bimbette, she headed to the last tent. A bone-thin, sun-browned mongrel with a patchy, once-white coat – now reflecting the colour of many puddles – sat licking a Kurkure packet. She had only one ear, which flopped sideways at an odd angle. One eye was clouded from an old injury; the other was sharp, amber and quietly defiant. A red thread around her neck acted as an ersatz collar.

The dog glanced up as Satyadarshi neared, her drumstick-like tail wagging like a metronome. She licked the outstretched hand, then rose shakily with a tilted gait. Satyadarshi knelt beside her, pulling out a Parle-G biscuit from her bag and offering it to Pari.

Of course, her name is Pari. Because irony runs faster than fleas.

Suddenly, a man approached, his UP-accented Hindi cutting through. 'Mangala told me a madam was asking about my Pari. What are you doing with her? See her collar? It shows she's mine. I won't let you take her away!'

Pari growled and edged toward her human. Satyadarshi sprang up, raising her hands in peace. 'I'm not here to take your ... Pari with me.' An idea stuck her. 'I wanted to get her vaccinated and checked by a vet.'

The man eyed her with suspicion. 'Why would you do that?'

'Pari's struck up a friendship with a pug,' Satyadarshi began, 'and his owner's an influencer – '

'Pug? What's that?' the man interrupted.

'The VodaTone dog?'

'Oh, yes. I've seen that tiny dog sniffing around my Pari.'

'Exactly. His name's Baby Bimbette, and his owner, Preia, wants to ensure Pari's healthy before they play together.'

'Oh, so the rich woman won't let my poor dog near her precious son?' The man eked out a bitter laugh. 'What's it to you? You want a cut?'

Another eureka moment struck her. 'No, no! I thought if we got her vaccinated and bathed, I could film a video of Pari and Baby Bimbette for an Instagram reel.'

'Papa, we'll come on the internet?' The man's son exclaimed eagerly.

'Chup raho!' The man raised his hand in mock anger. 'You won't take away my Pari, na? Everyone here adores her. We have little, but we pamper her. She's like my beti – she's my Papa ki Pari.' He glared at Satyadarshi. 'Don't cheat us, madam.'

Satyadarshi bit the inside of her cheek to stop herself from rolling her eyes. 'Yes, yes. My name is Satyadarshi. And you are?'

'I'm Banke Lal Yadav from Azamgarh in Uttar Pradesh,' he replied in halting English.

'And I'm Chote,' his son butted in.

'Yadav ji, let's take Pari to the vet,' she suggested, swiftly sending messages – one to Twa for a local vet's contact, one to Charan and the last to Jai.

I pray my idea works out ... Baby Bimbette, here we come.

A message from Jai rolled in.

You're a mad genius, Satyadarshi. But Baby Bimbette's heart is safe with you. And I need the entire story, pronto.

16

It was as if the gods were smiling down on Satyadarshi. The vet whose contact details Twarita had sent had a rare opening in his packed schedule – a cancelled appointment. He vaccinated Pari, administered anti-tick medications and sent her for a medicated bath.

Though her wallet felt noticeably lighter, a cleaner, fluffier Pari emerged, sporting a proper collar over the red thread and a purple leash tethering her to Satyadarshi.

She waited impatiently at the Horniman Circle Fountain, stealing glances at her watch every few minutes as Pari sat calmly at her feet. She had promised Yadav ji she would be back with his dog by 8:00 p.m., and it was already pushing 6:00 p.m.

Where were they? It all worked out in the end. Thank God that I'm dressed in decent clothes today and not in my usual uniform of black palazzos and a tunic. My purple dress will add some colour to the video. Along with Baby Bimbette and Pari.

Just as a sigh escaped her, she spotted Charan leading Baby Bimbette their way. Someone had dressed the pug in a red bow tie and a tuxedo, which hung loosely on his skinny frame. The moment he spotted Pari, he started whining and pawing the ground. Pari also let out a woof.

'Don't come too close, Charan,' Satyadarshi called. 'Wait till my friend arrives, then we'll shoot the video with the two dogs.'

'What do you plan to do, madam?' asked Charan.

Satyadarshi patted Pari on her head. 'I have a three-point agenda, Charan. One is to win back Preia's sponsors. Two, restore Baby Bimbette's health; and finally, maybe Preia could give this fluffball and her tubby bestie a chance at friendship.'

'And we are rolling ... action!' Charan announced with exaggerated flair. Baby Bimbette was nestled in Satyadarshi's arms, while Jai held Pari. The camera focused on her face as she got ready.

She exhaled, rolled her eyes at herself for the drama and launched into speaking.

'So, here's the story you didn't ask for but definitely need.' Charan panned the camera to Pari and Jai, who looked eager to escape.

'This is Pari. A street-smart stray dog, part-time site supervisor at a Colaba construction zone, with a résumé that includes dodging cars and living the best she can.'

Pari licked her nose, making her giggle. 'And that is Baby Bimbette. Pedigree pug, influencer-adjacent, Bisleri-drinking dog, who has more followers than me, my therapist and the municipal corporation combined.'

Jai edged closer, maybe for the frame, maybe not. She didn't ask. 'The two of them crossed paths despite class lines, kibble choices and wildly different hygiene philosophies. And still – it was friendship at first ... sniff.'

She paused dramatically. 'But, like in all great relationships, society stepped in. Preia, his human, forbade her brand-star from canoodling with an "outsider". Pari's human, a labourer from UP, declared, "Hands off my doggy!" Many others whispered, boys and girls can't be "just" friends.'

Jai knelt and released Pari, who padded over to Baby Bimbette. Satyadarshi continued, 'So, we did what any logical person would do.' The camera dramatically zoomed in on her face. 'We made a reel. Lights, love, two excited dogs and one hope ... '

Pointing at the two dogs running around, the camera obediently followed. ' ... That this video goes viral. Make *it* happen! Let's prove that a boy from a rich family can and will be friends with a girl from the slums. Just one request. No *Slumdog Millionaire* jokes, please.'

Jai gave an awkward wave just as Baby Bimbette launched into an enthusiastic sniffing spree. Pari flopped over in response, tail wagging like she'd just heard wedding bells.

'And cut!' yelled Charan.

'Well,' Satyadarshi muttered. 'That's one way to break the internet.'

St. George's Hospital was amongst the oldest hospitals in Bombay. As Satyadarshi waited for Niren Shadaj to arrive, her mind cartwheeled through last evening's events. The Baby Bimbette and Pari reel – now tragically, and publicly, shipped as 'BimRi' – had become an overnight internet sensation.

Sponsors swarmed Preia with contracts, and even Banke Lal started receiving offers – from biscuits to branded collars. Twarita joked that the two dogs displayed more chemistry than Jai and SD. But then the viewing statistics for the video did something no one could – shut her into silence.

But the biggest headache for Satyadarshi? Ragini – who happened to see the video. And her mother was gloating so hard, she could've floated over Bombay like a rogue helium balloon with a superiority complex. Smug, shiny and impossible to ignore. *And* seriously annoying.

It was a Herculean task, but Satyadarshi forced herself to concentrate on the unsolved case at hand.

Several of Laxmi Pancham's contacts had turned up dead – five in total, with only Mr Shadaj barely clinging to life. Mr Raag was still missing – no leads, no trace. Mr Shadaj, whose son she was meeting in a while, was stabbed three times. His children were contemplating taking him off the ventilator. All this made Satyadarshi wonder why she was even here.

I want to know if he also had a copy of the music book. But confirming that piece of information doesn't solve Ms Pancham's murder for me, does it? Am I barking up the wrong tree? Maybe I'm not meant for real cases like Laxmi Pancham's. Maybe Baby Bimbette-level investigations are all I'm good for.

A man in his early forties approached her, and she quickly stood to greet him. 'Satyadarshi? Hi, I'm Niren.'

'Hello, Mr Shadaj. It's good to meet you, though I'm sorry it's under these circumstances.'

'Thank you. Would you mind if we stepped across for a cup of tea? I need a break from the depressing hospital environment.'

They walked a few metres ahead and ordered tea from Sharma Snacks – which had a branch near the hospital – as they seated themselves on the wooden benches.

'I want to confess I asked people about you and about your reputation. When you first called me, I didn't know you from Adam, and I wasn't comfortable talking about Papa to anyone. From what I've heard, you're honest and trustworthy. But they didn't go into much detail. Before I go ahead, I need to hear from you – why did you leave the police force, Satyadarshi?'

She hid her surprise under her poker face, knowing honesty was her best chance. 'Police work is a forced marriage of honesty and corruption. Like a hole in your shoe sole – you may try to dodge the filth, but the gunk always seeps in. Rather than get sullied and compromise my morals, I rose as much as I could in my career. But when it came to pleasing my superiors by turning my face away from justice, I quit. People talk about glass ceilings, but there is also something called a morality ceiling, which all police personnel encounter in their careers.'

'I see. And there are no skeletons in your cupboard?'

She paused to take a sip of the extra-sweet but hot cardamom tea. 'If there are any, they are the honest kinds.'

Niren nodded to himself. 'Fair enough. Let me start at the beginning. Papa was found in his flat in Nora Bazar. His physiotherapist discovered the door ajar when she arrived for their morning session. When she entered, he was partially on the sofa, partially on the ground and bleeding profusely.'

He gulped his tea and crushed the paper cup in his fist. 'She called an ambulance immediately and then called me. If it weren't for her quick actions, we would have lost him then and there.' He exhaled. 'Not that it's been of any great help. Unless a miracle happens, we're going to lose him, anyway.'

'Did the police figure out why your father was stabbed?'

'As per the official reports, Papa surprised a thief during a robbery after his morning walk. He was undergoing physiotherapy for his frozen shoulder and would take a couple of rounds in the society. His watch and mobile were missing.'

'Nothing else was taken?'

'Surprisingly, a wad of cash – just about fifteen thousand rupees – in his cupboard was left untouched. A very sloppy thief, eh? Which robber stabs a man three times and then walks off with his watch and wallet? It seems rushed.'

'I'm sorry, Niren.'

Niren rubbed his moist eyes. 'Thank you. So am I. My mom suffers from dementia, and we moved her to a care facility. She doesn't remember Papa's death. And now I'm forced to lie to her, saying he will visit her soon.' Drawing a shaky breath, he asked. 'How can I help you, Satyadarshi?'

If Mr Shadaj's stabbing is connected to the same chain of deaths that I uncovered, through swars, through Ragamala illustrations – then maybe there was still time to stop the last one.

'If it is not too much of a bother, I want to visit your father's flat. I'm looking for a book like this one.' Satyadarshi held out her copy of the *Origin of Music Across Indian Temples* for him. The same one that has turned up around every victim so far.

Niren looked into his clasped hands as he thought. 'Let me arrange for someone to sit with him. But let's do it fast.'

❈

On the return journey home, as the fast local duelled with the wind en route to Dadar, Satyadarshi mulled over what she had learnt today.

Five senseless deaths. They seem to be connected, but I can't pinpoint their common trigger point. What joins them? The only obvious link that jumps out at me is music.

But why would someone kill – and kill so violently, so repeatedly – for music? And what makes it worthwhile for them to kill? A contract? No.

It can't be music. It has to be something else. Something I'm missing. Something I can't see.

When she had entered Mr Shadaj's house earlier, a metallic scent clung to the upholstery – like rust soaked in rain or old blood steeped in fabric folds. His sofa, once a pistachio-coloured suede, was now mottled with uneven blackish-red stains. The flat looked like a forced bachelor pad after his wife moved to the nursing home.

Dusty photo frames lay on a table near the television, which itself needed scrubbing. Her eyes took in the green walls that direly needed a fresh coat of paint. Magazines were stacked neatly in a stand, and a dog's bowl sat by the kitchen. Thankfully, the dog had moved in with Niren's family. Wilting plants peeked through the balcony door, adding to the sense of decay that lingered in the room. Even before Mr Shadaj's attack, the apartment had begun to give up on him.

Satyadarshi didn't have to look for the wall hanging. Suspended above the stained sofa was a now-familiar banner: green background, a seven-pointed star encircling a golden musical note, a peacock on one side and an eagle on the other. Red, gold, white, blue and other bright tassels hung below like silent sentries.

She had touched it, hoping it would leach its answers into her palms.

The train's shuddering motion snapped her out of the memory, and she found her fingers clenched around the music tomes. She exhaled sharply.

Enough. Sometimes, the only way to think clearly is to stop thinking. I'm going to make a conscious decision not to think about the case anymore.

Let me plan my tasks. Set a reminder to ping Dhrupad Mama so he can talk to Jai. I should ask Jai about music's connection to murder. I wish I could hire King Ashoka's Seven Unknown to help me out with my case.

No, brain! No more thinking about the case.

She plugged in her earphones and hit play. Rakesh Chaurasia's bamboo flute poured into her ears, and she let her thoughts scatter, finally, like feathers in the wind.

17

The next morning, Satyadarshi lumbered into the dining area but perked up when she found Dhrupad Mama there.

Contacting him was item number one on my to-do list.

Even though he was the nerd mother-ship (uncle-ship?), she had realized she now enjoyed a sudden tolerance for nerds. Especially if their name started with the letter 'j' and ended in 'i'.

Currently, her Uncle Dhrupad – nicknamed Paddu by Ragini, whose moniker was Ragu – was glaring at her mother.

Nothing new. A precursor to another fight. Hello, every day.

'Good morning, everyone! Mama, you are just the person I wanted to speak with,' she said brightly.

She was used to the siblings fighting amongst themselves – a by-product of two highly opinionated people. 'What are you guys fighting about today? Who slighted whom? And to what death-defying degree?'

'Your mother, as usual, is being mulish. All I've asked of her are a few of Baba's personal items – as mementoes. But the reigning queen here thinks she is the sole custodian of his belongings.' He turned towards Satyadarshi. 'You tell her,

Darshi. I have given up.' His lips curled in a bid to meet his chin, while Ragini appeared unmoved.

'Don't involve Darshi in our arguments, Paddu. I said I'll go through Baba's desk in the music room. Once I do that, I will *personally* call you and hand over the items you requested!' Ragini retorted.

'I've been hearing that for the last three weeks, Ragu! Our father died two months ago. What's holding you back from clearing up his room?' His eyes, flashing with controlled fury, raked over Ragini.

'Not everyone can compartmentalize one's emotions like you, Paddu. Baba's loss hit me hard. It's bad enough I have to use the music room to continue his classes and mine. But crossing his tiny bedroom makes it worse for me. I miss him so much,' said Ragini, swallowing as her voice caught on the last word.

'Let me do it then, Daddy's Darling Daughter!' Dhrupad glowered.

'No! You'll throw everything away. You don't care for his stuff. You never understood the reverence of music in our lives. When Aai died, you convinced Baba and me to let you "clean" the music room, and we know what happened. You sold her notes to the raddiwallah! Her notebooks with the original compositions,' cried Ragini.

Satyadarshi lay a hand on her mother's arm. 'Aai, I'll do it. And Dhrupad Mama can help, won't you? We won't throw anything away but place them into different piles so you can go through them later. Is that okay?' Ragini nodded gratefully while Dhrupad eked out a stiff nod.

She glanced at his quivering self. Satyadarshi's uncle was always coiled tighter than the Kachuachaap coils they used to burn to kill the mosquitoes in summer, but he seemed more tightly wound than usual. There was a hum in the room – an undercurrent she couldn't place. Satyadarshi cocked her head, but neither Ragini's nor Dhrupad's expressions gave anything away. Ragini gave her a grateful smile.

Hmm. Is the case making me read emotions that don't exist? Or under-read them?

'Great, then it's settled. Mama,' Satyadarshi turned towards Drupad. 'A friend of mine needs your expertise in writing his PhD dissertation – '

'Oho! Is this friend Jai? The same one with whom your videos have gone viral?' Ragini's eyebrows began dancing the samba.

Satyadarshi glared at her mother. 'Reel, not video. And one reel, not multiple. It didn't go viral because of me, but because of Baby Bimbette and Pari. Anyway, forget that – '

'But you're holding hands with him, and a romantic song is playing in the background!' Ragini persisted.

'Aai, the song is for the dogs. And Jai and I are *not* holding hands. We were standing next to each other so we could be in the same frame!'

Shaking her head, she turned to her uncle, whose raised eyebrows she ignored. 'My friend asked me if you could spare a few hours as he wants to pick your brain. Will the coming weekend work, or will you be travelling for work again?'

Dhrupad's pinched features tightened further. 'I'm free even now. I quit the ASI.' He scratched his wrist absently – a stress-induced tic Satyadarshi remembered.

The two women stared at him, all moments of jocularity lost instantly. 'Why did you do that?' croaked Ragini.

'I had creative differences with the unit.' A failing-to-appear-nonchalant shrug from Dhrupad answered no questions. 'I don't want to talk about it,' he mumbled.

'But you love working for the Architectural Society of India! You joined as an intern and never left,' exclaimed Ragini.

Reading the room, Satyadarshi intervened before another fight could break out. 'Thank you, Mama. I'll share your number with him, if that's okay with you.'

'You do whatever you want to do, Paddu,' said Ragini, returning to the previous topic, and waved her hands off him, literally. She addressed Satyadarshi. 'When should we call Jai home for dinner?'

Satyadarshi grimaced. 'Ignore her, Mama.'

'Affirmative,' was his gleeful response.

'Let me give you some context before you meet him, preferably before Aai interrupts us again. Jai read a paper of yours about the Travancore king and the Vishnu temple. He was mighty impressed with the quality and depth of your research, and he wanted to ask you a few questions regarding that. You guys can bond over history!' Satyadarshi said, shuddering.

'Yes, Paddu must get acquainted with Jai. Especially if he'll be a more ... permanent fixture in our lives.' She tapped Dhrupad on his arm. 'He's a nice guy. Brainy and handsome too! Do I sniff something fishy in the air, Darshi?'

Dhrupad and Satyadarshi both rolled their eyes at the beaming Ragini.

⌘

Having smoothed over the sibling stand-off, Satyadarshi skipped breakfast and caught a taxi to Matunga East, where she was due to meet her father, Raghuram. He was tapping his fingers on his wrist, slouching in front of Anand Bhavan. On spotting her, he gave her a quick hug.

'Satya, I'm in need of my morning coffee fix. I couldn't make it at home as I was out of coffee powder! The horror.' Clutching her hand, he half-dragged her inside. After plonking themselves on their usual bench, he beckoned the server over.

'Two masala dosais and two filter coffees. Fast!' urged Raghuram. 'Get the coffees first. And two more tumblers after we finish the dosai! Go! Go!'

'Appa, give the man a break.' Satyadarshi smiled at the nonplussed waiter, who ran to the kitchen.

Within minutes, two stainless steel dabara sets of piping hot coffee were placed on the white Formica table. Satyadarshi was immediately enveloped in the caffeine aroma, strong enough to rouse the dead.

Raghuram poured the coffee from the tumbler into the bowl and sipped like a man possessed – thankfully, soundlessly. Satyadarshi watched him, affection etched across her face as her father's eyes closed of their own accord as the caffeine rush hit his bloodstream. He inhaled deeply and greedily gulped a few more sips before slowing down. She felt his brown eyes linger on her face

'Ah! I feel like a human now. So, what is happening, Kanna? How are you? How is your mother?' Raghuram fiddled with the starched collar of his blue-chequered cotton shirt as he patted his forehead with a glaringly white, neatly folded handkerchief. Once done, he pocketed it in his loose, acid-washed jeans.

The glint of the overhead light reflecting off his watch – the black Titan – caught her attention. She eyed it, comparing it with the one she had barely glimpsed in Mr Dhaivat's flat.

'Not much, Appa. I'm swamped with work. Wrapped up a canine case, which came back like a boomerang. It was more fun the second time. I got to pet two dogs, and you know how I love them. Aai is doing well. Gandharva keeps her busy, and the music classes in the morning and evening are a blessing … for me.'

'Yes, you and your doggy prem. That's the reason your canine tooth exists.' He laughed as Satyadarshi stuck her tongue out at him. 'Your mother is extremely talented, and she could have gone – can still go – places with her singing if she had tried hard enough.'

'She has enough on her plate, Appa.'

'I know, Kanna. Baba also kept pushing her towards learning under Pandit Joshi, but Ragini … '

'Aai and Dhrupad Mama were arguing this morning,' she tried to divert the topic before she was lost in the debris of oft-heard complaints.

'What did the nincompoop want now?' Raghuram twirled his tumbler and finished his coffee while Satyadarshi nursed hers.

'I don't know the exact story, Appa, but I think he wanted some of Ajoba's personal items for himself, and Aai was resisting his attempts. Ajoba's death, though expected, still pulled the carpet from under our feet.' She held Appa's warm hands. 'I was confident that he would defeat cancer, especially since the last report had been so encouraging.'

'Yes, Satya. His death was … surprising. Did I tell you? He had called me the night before he died in his sleep. He wanted to hand over a box to me for safekeeping. Over the phone, Baba said that I was to keep it until he died and then give it to Ragini.'

'Oh! What happened to the box?' Satyadarshi asked, her mouth agape.

Raghuram waited for the server to place the masala dosai on their table with the hot sambar and chutney. 'I didn't get to meet him, Kanna. The morning I was to pick it up, he was already dead.'

'I've offered to clean his desk this weekend. If I find it, I will hand it over to Aai.'

'There were occasions where I think Baba had lost vital pieces of memory. He rambled a lot, Satya. Once he called me at midnight to recruit me for some covert operation, as he felt none of his children were up to the mark, especially Dhrupad.'

'Huh?' exclaimed Satyadarshi.

'Exactly. He said Dhrupad was too full of himself. He said the man had no reverence for music. And that he hated the entire matrilineal lineage of the Jaipur Gharana. It was a strange conversation. Made stranger when Baba termed him the "Urban Sita-less Ravan".'

'Sita-less Ravan? Why?' *My entire family is losing their marbles. How does that bode for me?*

'Well, if Ravan hadn't kidnapped Sita, he would've been barely distinguishable from the other kings of his time. His claim to fame was that one act. All his intelligence, all his smartness, couldn't prevent his fall, could they? So, Dhrupad was a Sita-less Ravan. Highly knowledgeable but partial to disaster.'

'Really? I can't relate to that side of Ajoba. To me, he was always a teddy bear who granted wishes.'

'Perceptions. Though he was that version for you, Satya, Baba was astute, and he taught me a lot in my life, and for that, I'm forever grateful. He pestered me to pursue my doctorate in history. I'm what I am today because of his faith and trust in me and my abilities.'

'Appa.' Satyadarshi tore a piece of the dosai and scooped up the spicy potato filling and chutney. She stuffed her mouth, chewing while speaking. 'Why did you and Aai separate?'

A curtain fell across her father's open face, and his hand paused en route to the sambar. He sighed.

'Satya, it's not my story to narrate. Ragini holds the reins to it. I made the mistake of opening my mouth once, but now I won't do it again.'

He tapped the edge of his plate with the spoon, then smiled a little too quickly. 'Anyway, enough of all this. Tell me about this new case of yours. So, did you have to wade through Dombivli's monsoon-dried gutters again? Did I tell you I used to stay there for a brief period before your Aai and I got married?'

Satyadarshi blinked. His tone was breezy, but the timing made her pause. 'No. Dombivli ... is Dombivli. The case is complicated, Appa. I'm at my wits' end trying to make sense of it.'

'I may be just a professor of history, but I can still help my baby girl with her problems, can't I? Let me know if I can assist in any way possible.'

'Of course, Appa.'

'The other day, I was so pleased when I heard a jugalbandi between Ustad Allah Rakha and Zakir Hussain. What a wonderful piece it was! All thanks to your YouTube. Thanks for introducing me to it. It has opened a whole new world for me.' He chomped happily as he signalled to the waiter for coffee.

When her train was stuck at a signal crossing, a thought – unbidden – crept into Satyadarshi's mind.

How did Appa know about my Dombivli trip?

18

The sun slanted through the tree branches at Dadar East as Satyadarshi walked home from the station. She thought of taking a cab but knew the benefit of walking. Besides getting her steps in, it cleared her mind. Relevant information bubbled up. Things slotted into place. And the answers revealed themselves.

But currently, her head throbbed from the weight of too many contradictions. Appa's apparent evasive answers. Why didn't he tell her about their split? About her Dombivli trip? About Dhrupad Mama – or 'Urban Ravan', as Appa had called him?

Sometimes she wondered if she was solving Laxmi Pancham's case, or sifting through her family tree and finding objects that didn't belong – or were senseless in their existence. She yearned for simpler days.

As she passed the chowki, she saw a cluster of constables huddled by the roadside tea stall. One of them clapped another on the back, laughing, as they sipped their tea and teased each other.

Something in the gesture – something in the way their

uniforms swayed, half-buttoned and familiar – pulled her sharply back in time. Even though she was stationed in Colaba, location barely mattered to the overall equation in a police station. They were identical; only the names of the places and people changed. The furniture, the fixtures, the attitude, the red tape and the injustice remained the same.

Her mind went back to the day when everything changed. It may not have been a single moment, but a string of moments that necklaced around her, cutting off the oxygen supply. Every doubt she had buried smouldered like suppressed evidence. Pushed down long enough, they resurfaced as truths, and those truths still burned her, even now.

And still shamed her.

Her pace slowed as her mind shuffled through the images like a gambler shuffling cards at a casino – ritualistic, restless, always hoping the next turn would change everything. But somewhere the knowledge roosted: nothing would change.

Three years ago.

The heat. The weight of her badge. The moment when her spine chose truth over survival. The truth, however toothless, decided to bite, chewing off a proverbial pound of flesh.

The press conference room at the commissioner's office was sweltering despite the air conditioning struggling in the background. The heat wasn't from the temperature, but from the bodies gathered there, the barrage of camera flashes and the tension that hung like a heavy cloud.

Satyadarshi stood behind the podium, her crisp khaki uniform chafing the back of her neck, her face unreadable. The nameplate over her breast still read 'Inspector Satyadarshi.'

Not for long, it seemed to her.

They had sent the official version to her that morning. It was everything she suspected, but it still felt like a sucker punch.

Victim was under the influence. No signs of foul play. Preliminary forensics align with the conclusion that the victim was not assaulted. She is using the law to frame her innocent husband, to slander his good name.

Only it wasn't true. Satyadarshi had the photographs, the eyewitness testimonies, the missing CCTV footage at the restaurant, the interviews with the broken parents, the fear in the victim's eyes … and the truth.

She had the truth.

She had her orders.

And Satyadarshi had a decision to make.

'I promise you will be promoted after this case,' her superior had said confidently, fingers drumming on the file open on his uncluttered desk. 'Keep your head down. Do the smart thing. You have a long way to go in the service if you learn a few tricks.'

But what was the smart choice? To be a good cop … or a good human?

She walked up and adjusted the microphone as multiple sets of eyes burned into hers. The journalists in front of her leaned in, smelling drama, fingers poised over their notebooks, phones ready to record.

The speech she had prepared burned the inside of her mouth. The words never left her tongue.

Her voice didn't break as she said. 'I have a statement.'

Then she read out the version they had handed her – clipped, cold and false. The speech she had prepared stayed inside, words tied by an official leash.

She couldn't recall the walk home that evening after duty – only the bitter aftertaste of defeat flooding her mouth.

The way other officers, constables, staff and journalists looked at her differently.

Admiration twinned with distance.

Later, her original file surfaced and spread. No one ever knew how. The press dug around, as they always did. Soon, her version of events was whispered in corridors, debated in newsrooms and then petered out. Not confirmed. Not denied.

Then the 'we are with you' calls dwindled to silence. Her boss assigned deadbeat cases to her. An inquiry was raised, as expected, about the leak. The report branded her impulsive, too emotional for the job, unfit for leadership – for police work.

Satyadarshi never corrected them. Sometimes silence killed from the inside. But she learnt and evolved.

In the whole rigmarole, what bothered her the most were the consequences. Life-altering ones that hit closer to home. Her misfortune didn't stay isolated; its tentacles spread like cancer, fed by gossip and rivals who thrived on their apparent disgrace. Ragini's concerts were cancelled. Ajoba's students stopped showing up. Appa's college forced him to go on a sabbatical. The whispers about 'that family' spread faster than any truth. The name their family had honed over years appeared tarnished.

And when Ajji's health declined that year, no one made the connection out loud, but it lingered – her decline too quick, too conveniently timed with the slander. Satyadarshi never spoke of that day again. Not fully. Not even to herself. Only Twarita made passing references to it, and even those were rare.

She left the force with silence stitched into her skin – one she still carried.

But what never changed was her family's unyielding support – Appa, Aai, Ajoba and Ajji. They had her back. And then Twarita joined the band of cheerleaders, her private circle of people who kept her alive.

And here she was, beginning to doubt that very band.

Satyadarshi turned the corner and saw her home. As always, the lights were switched on in the balcony. Ragini's silhouette moved past the window, probably humming something that might have been her favourite Raag Yaman – or perhaps something new.

Satyadarshi inhaled deeply, leaning against the metal society gate.

This case was not the same. She was not the same – but the feeling of standing alone at the microphone – still steady, still strong.

She pressed her fingers to her temple. 'Let's finish what

we started, Darshi. Seek the truth, and it shall set you free. Maybe this time it will,' she whispered.

And walked in.

19

Early the next morning, Satyadarshi sat cross-legged on the spotless floor of her office. She had given Twarita the day off.

Coloured pens, strings, glue and papers lay scattered around her. Her fingers were smudged with ink, and she gnawed on the pencil's end, her brows furrowed in concentration. She made a few additions to the paper, set the pencil down and held her magnum opus up.

Written neatly in different colours were all the people who were involved in the Laxmi Pancham case. Using cotton strings, she connected the various cards so that the relationship between each person became clearer. Strings snaked around the sheets like the tangled wires of Twarita's desktop computer.

I barely have any information about Mr Raag. He's the only contact of Ms Laxmi's I can't place. I need to dig; maybe he holds the cards to unravelling the mystery. Or *maybe not.*

Satyadarshi was pleased with herself. Sometimes the old-fashioned way of putting pen to paper was preferable to the digital world of laptops. When one sees the words, the brain kick starts itself into action and thoughts flow.

At that hour on a sunny Saturday morning, she knew exactly what information she possessed, who knew whom and how. This helped to clarify the hotchpotch in her head.

She peeked at her watch and decided it was time to clean up and head home. She had promised her mother she would clean up Ajoba's room tomorrow, even though the thought of it shredded her heart. But she had wrapped up her work faster than expected, freeing up the rest of the day.

Why wait until tomorrow? I'll tell Mama I did it a day earlier. She closed her eyes. *I need to do this for Aai. But I need to fortify myself first.*

Pushing her back against the desk, Satyadarshi let her gaze drift to the empty corner where Baby Bimbette had once napped after an impromptu 'investigation.' Her office was a place where dogs could roam without inhibition, since Aai wasn't around to suffer an allergic attack.

That day, she and Baby Bimbette had loads of fun. Twarita had joined in, too. The best thing about dogs, Satyadarshi had told Twa, was their noses – that wet, cold touch, followed by a lick, was the best kind of canine kiss!

A smile tugged at her lips, then slipped away as Jai's face edged into her mind. They hadn't spoken about the almost-kiss moment outside Pancham Puriwale.

Maybe it hadn't meant anything to him. Maybe it had. What did it mean to me?

We met that evening to shoot the BimRi reel, but too many people and too many activities didn't permit any chance for us to talk.

If Baby Bimbette hadn't shown up when he did ...

What would have happened? And how would I have reacted?

She rubbed her neck. *Dogs and timing. Both had an uncanny sense for ruining everything.*

Her phone buzzed with a meaningless message about home loans. As if she could afford to buy a flat in the city. With bank interest rates poised to break consumers' backs and property prices ensured they remained pipe dreams. Her eyes landed on the delete icon, but her finger hovered over a different name.

Jaya.

She hadn't renamed it to Jai because some part of her wasn't ready to deal with what the name might become – or what it already had.

Emotions are so confusing. Better not to have them at all than be caught in their quicksand.

Before she could talk herself out of it, she tapped the name and pressed dial. He picked up on the second ring.

'Hey,' she said, trying for casual, but it came out like someone testing a mic at a funeral. *Ugh. Whatever happened to my swag?*

'Hey,' Jai said. 'Are you okay, Satyadarshi? You sound weird.'

'Yeah, yeah. I'm fine.' She cleared her throat. 'Just ... ' She looked around the office. 'I finished work early and I ... um ... thought I'd go home. But then I didn't want to. So, I thought maybe ... if you're free?'

A pause. Then, warmth. 'I'm just finishing some reading at Kitab Khana. Want to meet me here?'

'Done,' she said, before her brain could raise an objection. 'Give me thirty. Or so.'

On the train to CSMT, she wondered if she was making a mistake; even though it didn't feel like one. It felt *right*. Was she falling back into a trap like a mindless masochist?

⌘

Stirring the kala khatta gola, Satyadarshi slurped the iced drink she had picked up near the Canon Pav Bhaji shop. She hoped that by now her tongue had turned purple. It was her favourite activity: to watch her tongue change colour.

Kala khatta gola was one of the few guilty pleasures in her life that had spilled over from childhood. It reminded her of the carefree days that all kids once enjoyed. And it helped her to stay in touch with her inner child. *If anything, I should stay away from my inner child and not increase our interactions,* she chuckled to herself as she sucked the sweet-and-sour flavour from the packed ice shavings.

Once the glass was empty, Satyadarshi pushed her shoulders back, slung her handbag over her shoulder and walked the few metres to Kitab Khana.

I wonder what Jai will think of my purple tongue. Why should I care? Ugh.

By the time she stepped into the bookshop, the warm scent of old and new paper and polished wood steadied her somehow. Jai was already there, flipping through a copy of *The Argumentative Indian* like he wasn't secretly waiting for her.

He looked up as she approached. 'Nice dress.'

She stuck out her tongue.

'Ooh, nicer tongue,' he said, his eyes holding hers for a beat too long. She smiled, and his smile widened at spotting her crooked canine.

'Don't let my bonhomie fool you. My mood still ranges from grumpy to mildly homicidal,' she warned.

'That's my favourite range.'

They browsed a bit at the bookstore. Jai found something obscure – and without a doubt, historical – and she picked up something absurd. Then, with unspoken ease, they drifted out and walked toward Kala Ghoda Cafe, weaving through the thinning crowd near Flora Fountain. The sun played peekaboo with the clouds, and an occasional breeze dried the sweat on her neck.

It was a relief when they slipped into the cool, dim-lit comfort of the cafe's exposed-brick interior. Over clinking cutlery, a shared cheese croissant and the smell of freshly brewed coffee, they settled into the kind of conversation that looped and meandered, touching on nothing urgent but feeling strangely vital.

After a while, a brief lull interrupted the flow. They both looked up at the same time, and their eyes met. Though they didn't speak of it, the moment Baby Bimbette had interrupted their almost-kiss hovered between them.

She stirred her coffee slowly and addressed the elephant in the room. 'If Baby Bimbette hadn't barked when he did,' she said, speaking to Jai's shoulder, unable to face him, 'do you think we would've … kissed?' she whispered.

Jai didn't look up right away. Then he exhaled. 'I think we were going to. But you stopped yourself before he even barked.' After a pause, he added. 'I know, I wanted to.'

She met his gaze. 'You're right. I excel at that – stopping things before they start.'

'Doesn't mean you should stop them,' he said. 'Not always, Satyadarshi. Sometimes certain things must happen for us to move ahead.'

She said nothing, letting the weight of it hang between them, safe in the soft clatter of cups and the occasional hiss of the coffee machine around them.

A part of her knew, even though she didn't say it aloud: had that kiss happened between Jai and her, she would've had no excuse left to pretend she didn't care.

'What does the rest of your evening look like?' Jai asked after a pause, reading her face, and changing the subject.

'I have to sift through Ajoba's stuff. I was headed home, but I thought I'd meet you if you were around … ' she faltered.

He placed his large, warm hands over her delicate ones. 'I'm glad you called me. And I'm happier we had this conversation. However awkward it may feel right now, it'll only settle things.' Jai linked his fingers loosely around hers. 'Don't let it change much. We're still friends, and I still enjoy meeting you. Don't stop that, okay?'

She smiled, but didn't quite know what to say, so she nodded.

When Satyadarshi reached home, she was glad Aai was out shopping. After meeting Jai, instead of her emotions settling, they kept churning on the return train journey.

And just like that, the weird quotient for this case hit new highs. She washed up and changed into yoga pants and an oversized T-shirt, before making a beeline for the music room, where her grandfather's desk waited patiently.

At the threshold, she paused for a minute as memories flooded her – Ajoba playing horsey with her squealing on his back; Ajoba chanting a shloka when she was sick, caressing her feverish forehead; Ajoba and Aji attending her first concert. Her grandfather crying openly while Ajji sat with a stiff upper lip. *She was quite a character,* a smile touched her lips.

As she stepped inside, she thought, *Memories are funny. While they make us buoyant, they also press down on our chests until we can't breathe. Bittersweet.*

On her cell phone, she put on Zakir Hussain's playlist. She'd need the extra boost his music could provide. Fine dust had collected all over Ajoba's precious table. His leather-bound books appeared forlorn for lack of company. She didn't touch the books but made a mental note to dust them once she was done.

At the corner of the room, a large window let in diffused sunlight, illuminating the dancing dust motes in mid-air, as if their colonies had claimed the room. Ajoba's desk stood beside it – a heavy, polished teakwood table. His black ergonomic chair with its embroidered cushion was pushed against it at an angle. The cushion was Satyadarshi's gift to him on his seventy-eighth birthday. She picked up the multicoloured compressed-cotton cushion and brought it to her nose, inhaling deeply.

Satyadarshi could still smell her grandfather's familiar spicy aftershave scent and Brylcreem pomade. For a moment, it grounded her like a warm hug, before withdrawing its support and letting her crumble.

Got. To. Keep. Moving.

She slumped into the chair and began to empty his desk. The drawers contained his daily schedule and several diaries. She added those to the must-stay pile. There were several loose papers that appeared to be bills and receipts. Ajoba was old-fashioned and, much against her wishes, still took printouts of not only receipts but also the bills. Satyadarshi placed the bills in the can-go pile, and the receipts in the must-stay section.

Working feverishly, she cleared the desk. The two heaps seemed to be competing in a silent battle of bulk. She quickly assessed the file cabinet along the desk; it would take about an hour, maybe more.

It's time for a change in the sequence of chores.

Satyadarshi rose and walked up to the bookshelves that

spanned half the wall, carrying a feather duster she found tucked under the desk. She removed each book, dusted it and gently placed it back. Some books were like long-lost friends, some were strangers. In the last remaining section, she came across stacked albums.

At least a break in the monotony of everything.

She picked up the entire lot and plonked herself on the small cream love seat with its cheerful rainbow cushions. Reliving Ajoba's memories through the black and white, then sepia-toned and faded colour photographs occasionally triggered a chuckle or a moan.

Dhrupad Mama's retro 70s look – with his sideburns and elephantine collars – made her burst into laughter. His flared bell-bottoms were a hoot! She could barely relate the man in the pictures to the one she knew now. *When did the easy spring of youth tighten into a weary coil?*

Ajji and Ajoba's wedding pictures showed them standing like mannequins, side by side. She wondered which colour saree Ajji had worn, picturing vibrant silks and subtle embroidery. *I wish I had asked these questions when she was alive. Or Ajoba.*

A bunch of photos stacked behind a sleeve showed her grandfather with a ridiculous hairstyle. It was probably Aai's fifth birthday; balloons were tacked to every wall as Ajji bent over the homemade cake, smiling Ragini in her arms, while Dhrupad stared at the cake as if he'd devour it.

People were scattered around the table, many caught mid-conversation when the picture was clicked. Satyadarshi wondered who the photographer was. She was about to flip to the next set when her eyes snagged on a detail. One laughing face in the corner of the frame, caught mid-gesture, half-lit, yet oddly familiar.

Satyadarshi frowned, bringing the photograph closer. The smile, the curve of the chin, the eyes that seemed to sparkle even in faded colour.

Her grip on the photo tightened, bending the edge. She could feel her pulse thrum against the paper.

No, it couldn't be.

But when she leaned in, the blur sharpened into recognition. A younger woman, her hand resting lightly on a boy's wrist – a very young Hariesh.

The woman was unmistakable now.

Laxmi Pancham.

She was chatting with Ajoba, who was mostly out of the frame.

It's Laxmi – a very young Laxmi, but her nevertheless. Ajoba and Ajji knew the Panchams? I didn't see THAT coming for sure. Wow! Small world.

None of the other pictures unveiled anything new, so Satyadarshi stuffed them back in place and replaced the albums after dusting them.

A few of these pictures can be given to Mama for remembrance's sake.

As she bent to wipe the last shelf, a pocket-sized album caught her eye. It contained Ajoba's office party pictures – in colour! Some were taken in this very room. It was amusing to see nothing substantial had changed in the music room for decades.

The last snapshot, however, made her freeze.

Her grandfather sat on an uncomfortable sofa that preceded the current loveseat. He held a tanpura, his long, shapely fingers curled around its neck. On the wall behind him hung the wall hanging Satyadarshi had seen in almost all the victims' houses, except Ms Madhyama's.

An elephant carried the seven-pointed star enveloping the golden musical note in its trunk, while an eagle hovered above against a multicoloured banner. Red, golden, white, blue and other tassels floated down its flanks, completing the image.

Satyadarshi stared at the picture, her eyes widening. *What the actual—?*

This was the wall hanging that connected the senior citizens together – along with the music book that Satyadarshi knew had originally belonged to Ajji.

What the heck was happening?

Dumping the album on the floor, she sprinted to the stubby cabinet and flung its metal doors open – the last unexplored bastion. Loose papers, half-filled notebooks with music compositions and other writings cluttered the cabinet.

In a Bata shoebox – iconic red, now faded – lay random papers and a clunky object wrapped in a grey pouch. The papers appeared to be letters that were sent to Ajoba over the years.

Nothing of relevance here.

Among the sheets was a ragged, torn piece of paper. A letter, in her grandfather's spidery handwriting. Well, a letter would be a misnomer. It appears to be part of a letter. A paragraph or two of it.

> … me deeply. He isn't the man I thought he was. The man I thought I knew. I've been deceived into thinking that the problems he faced had been treated and were in no way a hindrance to his life. But the mask of civility that he dons has been torn, and the person inside is a monster. And the bitter truth stings. Because I am integral in shaping him into the man he is now. But I never suspected anything was amiss. It's worse than I had ever anticipated. I'd like to warn my Ragini against him. As he may cause mischief. Probably has started.
>
> I'm already weakening. The wretched cancer has me in its evil clutches, but I can't see my daughter nor my Darshi suffer. Even in the state I am in, I must take the correct action. The right step. I'm scared of what he might do. Of what he is capable of doing. Yes, I need to safeguard them. I will take action to hide the identities of the …

The letter ended abruptly. She turned the half page over to see if anything was written behind it, but it was blank. Only the imprint of the ink showed through.

Who was Ajoba alluding to when he said he must protect Aai and me?

Appa's words from their meetings wandered across her mind like a half-forgotten refrain. *Baba was astute, and he has taught me a lot in my life, and for that, I'm forever grateful. He badgered me to pursue my doctorate in history. I am what I am today because of his faith and trust in me and my abilities.*

Was Ajoba referring to Appa? Why would Appa harm Aai and me? Why did he scare Ajoba?

Satyadarshi unwrapped the pouch to reveal a Nokia phone – the one with buttons and the iconic snake game. *Damn the snakes! Always popping up.* She examined the phone. *A hidden cell phone? Why?*

Her instincts were in mutiny, and her 'spidey sense' was tingling. The battery was dead, but its charger was still connected to the phone's port, its wire dangling from the box. She unplugged the Alexa Dot and plugged the other end into the socket.

The charging icon appeared on the phone's screen. When she pressed the start button, the phone hummed and started. She immediately checked the call logs, but they had been wiped clean. The network sign, the three bars, lit up on the right-hand side of the small screen.

With her hands shaking, Satyadarshi entered her number into the phone. It felt weird to actually press keys instead of just tapping them with her fingertips, and she made a few mistakes before getting it right. The call started to connect and went through.

Her own phone rang. She'd placed it on the desk while she flicked through the albums. She got up from the floor, her knees cracking and protesting the constant up-and-down movement.

She picked up the trilling phone. On the screen, instead of an unknown number, a name flashed.

Mr Raag calling.

20

Stuffing her sinking heart back into its original place, Satyadarshi examined the Nokia phone. It was a mostly empty shell. Call logs were blank, and so was the message inbox. Satyadarshi checked the draft folder and found a message, though it had no sender, just the content.

He has stumbled upon our network's secret. We need to be aware that he may come knocking on our door any day now. Initiate Plan B.

Was Ajoba Mr Raag? What was happening? She examined the other papers thoroughly. They were a printout of a list of books issued from a library in the last three months.

1. *Undercover Poisons* by Dr Venkat Mourthy
2. *When Drugs Mimic Natural Death* by Maura Chaps
3. *It Is Homicide Only If You Are Caught* by Simpson-O

The rest were books about travel and other mundane topics.

What a strange set of books to check out from a library!

Satyadarshi flipped to the second of the three stapled pages. The second one was again a list of educational books. The last page had barely a paragraph on it.

> The Indian Library levies a fine of Rs 500 on Prof. Raghuram Iyer for misplacing the book assigned to him. Prof. Iyer has failed to return the book despite repeated reminders.

It was Appa's library card. It was a printout of the list of books *he* had checked out.

Satyadarshi placed a hand over her spinning head. Just a few hours back, everything had settled in her mind. Everything had been in its place. And now, like a violently shaken snow globe, everything in her mind was muddled up and murky. And even when the snowflakes settled, nothing remained in its original position.

Fathers suspected to be killers. Grandfathers turning out to be related to victims ... and their murderers. It felt surreal. She pinched herself on the inner arm and yelped in pain.

I'm making a quantum leap here. Appa is a man of history. He's someone who believes in human rights, even for lizards – how can he grievously harm another human? No. This is atrocious. Ajoba was mistaken. Appa is good. Appa is kind. He's the blue-checks-wearing, French-beard-growing coffee hound.

Satyadarshi covered her face with her icy hands as she sank into the black chair, her body crashing onto the rainbow pillow. In a flash of anger, she retrieved the cushion, and with her eyes still closed, she threw it with all her might. The feather-light cushion didn't sail far, and neither did it lessen Satyadarshi's frustration or guilt.

It landed lopsidedly on the cream loveseat, camouflaging itself amongst its rainbow-coloured brethren. Her eyes tracked its trajectory and eventual settling, then shut again as her fingers curled into fists. Satyadarshi dumped everything into her backpack and bolted.

Appa is not a murderer. Ajoba doesn't come out and say it. And to whom was he writing the letter? It could be a prank. Ajoba enjoyed playing pranks. Yes, exactly. That's what it was – a stupid prank. Ajoba was a prankster.

The rational voice in her mind reared its ugly head.

The lady doth protest too much, methinks.

Satyadarshi was exiting the house when she crashed into Ragini, who carried bags bulging with groceries.

'Hey, when did you come home, Darshi? Help me with these heavy bags. Where are you rushing now? What happened? Is everything okay?' Ragini asked, anxiety clouding her features as she dumped the shopping bags on the floor.

'Nothing is the matter, Aai. Just remembered a detail about my case and wanted to check it out. I'll see you later,' replied Satyadarshi, amazed at her ability to sound and behave normally even when her world was crashing down.

Sprinting across the leafy roads, the beautiful trees had no effect on cooling Satyadarshi's racing mind. She spotted an empty taxi and boarded it. 'Bandra.'

'Bandstand, kya madam?' grunted the taxi driver.

'Yes.'

The flashing scenery, the traffic snarls, the roadside hawkers and the signals glowing all shades of red, yellow and green – Satyadarshi saw all of them during the journey and saw none of them. She disembarked from the taxi and paid the driver.

In a daze, she walked up to the promenade and found an empty concrete stone slab – not an easy feat on a Saturday early evening – and slumped on it. People milled around her, laughing, jogging, eating and having a good time. Satyadarshi's eyes took in the faces of the happy revellers, and in that instant, she felt very alone in the crowd.

It was high tide; the waves, relentlessly and tirelessly, crashed onto the sandy shore – much like the thoughts that overwhelmed Satyadarshi. The sea mist jolted her out of her mind funk. The left side of her brain took over, organizing the information – slotting it into correct boxes, sorting the wheat from the chaff. As the cogs turned in her brain, her emotions calmed, and Satyadarshi could breathe freely.

Analysis was what she was best at. She closed her eyes and breathed in the salty air.

Everything can be resolved when I speak to Appa. It could be just a simple misunderstanding. Whipping out her mobile, she dialled his number, but the call went unanswered. *Maybe he's in a class. Appa will call back. He always does.*

Her mental monologue was interrupted by a familiar, deep voice. 'Satyadarshi? What are you doing here? Are you stalking me? Again?'

Satyadarshi's eyes looked up from her lap to crash into Jai's quizzical gaze. 'Huh?' was all her overwrought brain could manage.

Jai, tall as ever, had changed into olive-green shorts. Sweat poured down his body, and he stared back at her. His white dry-fit T-shirt clung to his muscular chest, revealing its barrel shape.

Breathing hard, Jai bent towards her, his hands on his knees. Satyadarshi's eyes trailed a bead of sweat as it made its way down his sinewy, lean arms, joined others at his knee, and waltzed down his take-my-breath-away shapely calves.

When they met a few hours back in town, he was wearing his usual fare – casual trousers and a button-down shirt. The only other time she had seen him dressed differently was when they met at Prithvi. Her overburdened brain was finding it difficult to connect this ... this sweaty hunk with mussed-up hair to the neatly combed, nerdy Jai.

A sweaty hunk who said, 'Satyadarshi? Are you okay? You're looking through me as if you don't know me. I'm Jai, remember? We just had coffee a few hours ago – okay, four hours ago.'

Satyadarshi stopped wool-gathering and spun a cogent sentence. 'I didn't expect you here, and I didn't even recognize you ... '

Jai straightened as he laughed, attracting the eyes of the women around them like iron filings to a magnet. 'Ah, yeah. But I recognized you, even without your purple tongue. I run here whenever I need a break from studying.' His fingers slicked back a lock of hair from his forehead, and a collective sigh went through the crowd. 'Can I join you?'

Satyadarshi scooted over as Jai sat with a grimace. 'My left knee acts up from time to time – an old injury. What are you doing here? You looked very pensive a while back.'

Satyadarshi nodded. *Running into Jai twice in one day short-circuited my worry loops. It's funny what mild attraction and familiar banter can do to a scrambled brain. They can dissolve tangible worries.*

'I needed a break too. And there's nothing more powerful than watching waves make mincemeat of the shore, is there?' she said.

'Yes. And very poetic too. This is what's missing in Pune – a beach. Usually, I prefer mountains, but seas make a compelling argument in their favour, don't they? Though if Pune had a beach, it would be as muggy as Mumbai,' Jai unstrapped a water bottle from his right shoulder, took a sip and offered it to Satyadarshi. 'Do you want some?'

'No, thanks. You forget I'm a Mumbai-kar; I carry a lifetime stock of drinking water with food and entertainment whenever I travel,' she joked, pointing at her backpack lying by her side.

Jai raised his hands in apology. 'Sorry.' His laughter felt like a balm to Satyadarshi's frayed nerves.

She leaned back, her arms outstretched behind her. 'I always wanted to ask you this question. How come you call me by my full name?'

'Because it *is* your full name.' He cocked his head at her, quizzically.

Satyadarshi chuckled. 'Yeah, but no one ever calls me by it. Except officially, of course. It's always Satya, or Darshi or even SD!'

'Well, now you know someone who does call you Satyadarshi. Come on, let me buy you an iced coffee. This time it's my treat and no arguments over it!' Jai stood up and offered his hand to Satyadarshi, who grasped it, and he hoisted her up.

She was surprised at how her hand disappeared in his. And how safe it made her feel.

⁂

It was never about the music.

Everyone thought it was.

They cloaked themselves in swars and ragas, in tanpuras and taals, pretending that their pursuit was sacred, noble. That their devotion made them pure, untouchable – as if the sheer act of singing made them better than the rest.

No.

It was about control.

Power.

Who got to sit in the centre of the circle. Who got to be remembered. Who decided which notes survived.

They dressed it up as heritage and fed the children early on with pretty lies: your voice is a gift; your inheritance is sacred. Some swallowed it whole and grew up thinking they were the chosen ones.

Convenient, wasn't it?

They didn't want guardians. They wanted disciples. They wanted emotion, surrender, acceptance. They didn't care about the brain's wiring, or its training. No space for certain kinds of minds.

So, the quiet ones watched. They waited. They learnt.

Let them dismiss what they could not see. Let them keep singing, unaware of what shadows were listening. Because knowledge has a way of returning to the one who seeks it. Music wasn't divine. It was a map. Notes weren't feelings. They were codes. And codes can be broken.

They underestimated what lay outside their circle – what didn't bow and what didn't belong. But it listened. It read. It studied what they ignored – the footnotes, the symbols, the buried stories, the things between the swars.

They wanted lineage? They would get a legacy. In blood. In silence. In the absence of song.

Let them try to sing their way out of this.

Silence can be killing.

No one better than the listener to know this.

21

Satyadarshi and Jai ambled towards the Barista Cafe, which was a few hundred metres ahead of Bandstand. Their arms occasionally touched as they walked, and each time, a new set of buzzing triggers shot up her spine.

At the cafe's door, Satyadarshi laid her hand on Jai's arm. It was slick with sweat but firm under her fingers. 'Can we walk while we drink? I don't want to go in. It's too stuffy.'

Jai raised his eyebrow. 'Sure. Why don't you sit here? I'll go and get the drinks. Do you want something to eat?'

She shook her head, and he went inside. The whoosh of machine-cooled air felt good for a while. Satyadarshi stood under the cafe's swirling red umbrella, staring at the growling sea while she waited.

Spending a few minutes with Jai had calmed her down, and she felt more in control of her situation.

What worries me is why an external person's presence is what made me forget for a while. I don't want to be dependent on anyone. I learnt this the last time around. I take care of myself the best.

Jai returned, holding the tall paper cups. 'I didn't get straws.'

'That's okay. Shall we walk towards the sea?'

'Of course.'

They sipped in companionable silence, with Jai stealing glances at her, but she kept her head down. Satyadarshi slurped her way through her drink, and when they reached the promenade, they sat on a slab. The slanting rays of the setting sun cast them in a golden light.

Jai turned towards her after finishing his drink and observed her for a while. She watched whatever was on her face register on his.

Finally, he asked, concern etched in his voice. 'Are you okay, Satyadarshi? Did clearing your grandfather's desk upset you? Do you want to talk about it?'

Satyadarshi raised her chin towards the fading light. 'I'm better now, thanks to you. But no, maybe later.'

Whatever Jai was going to say was cut off by a yellow Labrador Retriever who ran towards them and buried his nose into Jai's crotch. Jai glanced at her and the dog, arching an eyebrow with a goofy grin on his face. His human came huffing and puffing, mouthing apologies galore.

'I'm so sorry! Biscuit just escaped from the leash and started running. Did he hurt you? Oh my God, did he lick you?' the owner asked, trying to separate her dog and his tongue from Jai. Her pixie cut stuck out in rebellious little tufts as she tried to control Biscuit. She fell back as the labrador changed his track and dug his wet nose into Satyadarshi's stomach, making her giggle.

'Hey, it's okay,' laughed Jai. 'We have dogs at home, so I'm used to them – and their strange behaviour!' He patted the Labrador, who sat on its haunches, offering its droopy, silky ears for a scratch, and Jai obliged.

'Phew! I'm so glad. Not everyone loves a big slobbering dog breathing down their face. Now that Bisc has made friends with you, get used to him trotting over every time he spots you!' she huffed, trying to catch her breath between sentences. 'I'm Natalie!' she concluded after a long breath.

Satyadarshi and Jai introduced themselves, and after pampering Biscuit thoroughly, they bade him a reluctant farewell. He trotted off, tongue lolling, with his human.

Satyadarshi leaned back on the stone slab and turned to Jai, 'Dogs are the best! I didn't know you had one at home,' she said.

Jai stretched his hands behind him, mimicking her pose. 'Yeah. We have two in Pune – a Boxer and an Indie – Misal and Pav. Pav is spicier than Misal, who's as bland as can be.' He whipped out his phone and showed her their pictures.

'How adorable are their names! How old are they? Appa and I wanted a dog, but Aai is allergic, and with her singing career, we could never risk it. I plan to get a Labrador later in life. Even if Aai protests!'

Jai chuckled. 'Adopt instead of buying; that's my suggestion. Pav is four years old and Misal is seven.'

They lapsed into silence, and case-related thoughts once again weighed on Satyadarshi's mind. Jai touched her hand lightly. 'You appear tense again.'

She let out a long sigh. 'This case has been very tiring for me, Jai. Every time I think I've resolved something, I crash into a concrete wall of more questions. It's the reason I needed a break. And a change of scenery.'

'Is there any way I can help you, Satyadarshi? I don't know much about detective-ing and related stuff, but I can act as a sounding board if you're interested.'

'Thanks, but I can't disclose information because of confidentiality agreements. Tell you what – why don't you distract me with your research? I'll zone out, and maybe the answer will come to me?' Satyadarshi flashed a cheeky grin at Jai.

'So you *do* think I'm boring, huh? Chalo, doesn't matter, at least you think about me.' Before Satyadarshi could react to that comment, he continued. 'I don't mind being the Watson to your Sherlock. As you know, my dissertation topic deals with ancient India, and I'm focusing on the legacy of King Ashoka – I find him very intriguing.'

He pushed his errant lock back. 'When he formed Ashoka's Unknown Seven, he named them after the seven swars – Sa, Re, Ga, Ma, Pa, Dha and Ni – relying on the logic that if he chose musicians to head his teams, their constant meetings would not raise eyebrows, since artists often had mehfils or jamming sessions.'

'Wait, wait – he named spies after musical notes?'

Jai gave her a tapli on her head. 'You expected code names like Cobra and Panther? This is India. We do things differently.'

She signalled for him to carry on.

'Ashoka probably had no idea how far the concept would travel or how much it would benefit others.'

'How do you remember all this? Did you swallow a book?' Satyadarshi asked in wonder. 'On a serious note, how would it benefit others?'

Jai's full lips parted, and he winked at her before continuing. 'Many kings employed the septet to safeguard their treasures. In fact, the Travancore king relied heavily on their services. The Vishnu temple consists of six kallaras – or vaults – that have been unearthed.'

'Could there be more?' Satyadarshi interrupted.

Jai shrugged. 'Who knows? Though I don't think so. These are the ones that we know of. Out of them, A, C, D, E and F have been opened and their treasures counted. It's the Bharatakkon Kallara – or Chamber B – that holds all the mystery.'

'But does this connect to King Ashoka? The vaults? Was the treasure King Ashoka's?'

'Wait, my eager beaver. I'm getting there.' He tapped her head again.

'Faster. Remember homicidal tendencies,' she said with a grin, flashing her sleuthing fang.

A flash of a smile crossed Jai's face, and he shook his head. 'Vault B allegedly holds the greatest treasure known to man.

Out of its three doors, the last one still stands sealed. Two cobras guard the door and there's no apparent way to open it – no knobs, no slits.'

Satyadarshi hit her forehead. 'That's where the snakes come from! I kept thinking of them. Please continue.'

His lips quirked. 'The myth says the king of Travancore sealed the door with a Naag Paasam and only a specific mantra can open it.'

'Uh-huh! So, like the duo of Tansen and his daughter singing Raag Deepak and Megh Malhar to light and douse the fire respectively, your mantra can open a door that's never opened since it was sealed,' scoffed Satyadarshi.

'Laugh all you want, my dearest detective friend, but that's exactly how it's supposed to play out.'

'So how come, in all these years, if people knew the mantra, no one could chant it and open the door?'

'Oh, they have tried. How they have tried!'

'But none succeeded.'

'Yes. That's because the secret was split into seven parts. Each incantation has to be sung in one raga at a certain time. And since the names of the septet have been lost in the annals of history; those who've tried don't know which raga or order to sing in for the Garuda Mantra to open Vault B.'

Satyadarshi's feet itched; she stood up abruptly. She stared at Jai, who looked back in puzzlement.

'What? What did I say?'

Ragas. Order. The swars. The tassels. Animals. Books. Wall hangings.

Her hands tightened around the paper cup, crushing it until a few drops spilled onto her fingers, though she didn't notice. *It wasn't music. It was code.*

'Repeat what you just said, Jai,' she said.

'Oh ... kay. They don't know the ragas or the order in which to sing the Garuda Mantra that will open the doors of Vault B. Are you okay, Satyadarshi? You look very pale.'

Confusion reflected in Jai's eyes as his hands slipped around her waist to keep her steady.

Satyadarshi slumped against him, muttering. 'That's the connection. The glue that holds everything together. Or unravels it. The Garuda Mantra. That's why it was written in every book. And that's why the markings were made to indicate the raga names. Why couldn't I figure that out? I've studied the theory for years. How could I not see the connection?' She buried her face in her hands and screamed softly.

'Satyadarshi, will you tell me what's going on?'

'Wait. Let me think, just a minute. So ... could it be that Ms Laxmi, Mr Shadaj and others were all part of the septet?'

She turned towards Jai and held his wrist urgently. 'Jai, tell me more about the Sa Re Ga Ma Dha Ni stuff you mentioned earlier.'

'Arrey, you're the musician. You know more than I do.'

'Humour me. Please.'

Jai took one look at Satyadarshi's determined face. Her brown hair was tied up in a loose ponytail; her kohl-lined eyes and her pert nose were set in an expression that didn't leave him with much choice. Her tiny diamond earrings caught the glare of the farewell rays of the sun. But what warmed his heart was her crooked canine tooth. Still, Jai couldn't be distracted for long, because all those features also reflected a deep impatience. So, he continued.

'Here's what I know. Essentially, the seven swars are formed by the sounds and colours of nature. Like Sa – short for Shadaj – comes from the sound of a peacock and the colour green. Ga or Gandhar – the bleating of a goat – is brown, sometimes even a golden hue. Pa or Pancham, from a nightingale's song, is blue. You get the drift, right?'

'Tell me more.'

As Jai spoke, memories sparked and fused in her mind, whizzing past fragments of information and snapping into place, until they formed a chain – a chain of light, of Eureka moments. Each image flickered like a reel in an old slide projector.

Red, golden, white, blue ... always those tassels. Always the eagle. But the animals – they changed.

Laxmi Pancham's apartment. *Threads of red, golden, white, blue and other colours adorned a seven-pointed star embracing a musical note on which a nightingale and an eagle were perched, pecking at it with their beaks. Blue. Pa for Pancham.*

Rishabh Chopra's house. *A cow replaced the nightingale, and along with the eagle, they nudged the star against a cherry-red background. Red. Re for their middle names, Rishabh. Of course.*

Suhel Dhaivat's bedroom. *A yellow wall hanging with a horse. Dha for Dhaivat. I knew that yellow was too perky.*

Mr Priyam Gandhar's living room. *A brownish banner with a goat. Gandhar comes from Ga – how did I miss that? I had thought about swars before, hadn't I? And yet the name hadn't clicked until now.*

Mr Shadaj's flat. *Green background and a peacock. Shadaj – Sa.*

Even though, I didn't spot the wall hanging in Ms Madhyama's bungalow, I did get the book.

Lastly, their music room. *A multicoloured cloth showing an elephant carrying the same seven-armed star in its trunk while an eagle hovered above it – the one hidden in Ajoba's desk. Ni for Nishad. Ajoba's name.*

She blinked, her breath catching. *It's all there. The animals weren't decorative. The colours weren't for aesthetics. They were clues – the keys. Sa. Re. Ga. Ma. Pa. Dha. Ni. The case started with Pa for me, but it began much, much earlier. Probably with Mr Shadaj's stabbing.*

Satyadarshi jumped up, grabbed Jai's hands. 'Jai! You're a genius. I can't thank you enough. Next time, the coffee's on me. Got to rush!'

Before leaving a bewildered Jai on the pavement, Satyadarshi rushed back and hugged him tightly. 'I owe you one.' She planted a gentle kiss on his jaw, right at the corner of his mouth, then sprinted off. 'I'll call you soon!'

All this time, I thought I was following a killer. Turns out, I've been following my own blood.

I can't believe it. My Ajoba – Mr Balwant Nishad Phadke.

Mister Balwant Nishad Phadke.

Mr Know-it-all.

Mr I-have-all-the-data-in-my-grasp.

How gratifying it was to see his face when he realized what I had done. How understanding – although late – rushed through his bloodstream like the untraceable drug I had laced his tea with.

The old man's mouth had formed a moue of disbelief, had attempted to speak, to chastise, but ended up in a grimace as his heart collapsed. He died knowing his murderer. He died knowing it was his time.

He died knowing it was me.

He died *knowing.*

A smile broke across his face as he relived those precious moments. The only regret he had was that the man had taken his secrets to the pyre with him. Despite every scheme he devised, every torture he inflicted, Mr Encyclopaedia had not broken.

Tonight, the black cloth was spread across the floor, a straw doll with a round head bound in red thread lying at its centre. Crude, almost laughable in appearance, until you saw the name scrawled across its chest. He didn't need a likeness. A name was enough. The sound carried the essence; the syllables were the soul.

Satyadarshi.

Beside it, a copper lota brimmed with water thickened by ash. He dipped his fingers in, smearing a stripe across the doll's head. He traced the letters with his ash-stained fingertips. Then, gently – almost reverently – he held it in his palms.

'Like an ant that has just found her wings. So easy to crush mid-flight,' he whispered.

His chant rasped, fractured, like something pulled from a grave. With every syllable, his hand tugged at the red thread knotted around the doll's throat.

One knot. Two. Three. Each one tighter. Each one closer to silence.

Until the doll's head lolled free.

Victory was not just in vaults or mantras. It was in the hush after the last breath. And soon, she would learn it.

The black Titan watch on his wrist blinked the time. He had finished the ritual exactly on schedule. The stars themselves aligned in his favour.

Everything as planned.

He could almost see the doors of Vault B grind open, the mouths of those around him matched the motion – eyes wide with awe. Their hero worship.

It is time.

Swaha.

22

It was past ten when Satyadarshi walked into her office. She hadn't planned to be there. After she met Jai, she didn't want to go home.

Maybe she didn't want to answer Aai's questions. Or catch sight of Ajoba's framed photo on the wall, now transformed from a proud relic to a silent accusation. Maybe she just didn't want to be alone with her thoughts, where no one could argue back. And punish herself with unfettered questions about Appa.

She chose what felt like the best option at that moment, she messaged Twarita and begged her to come to the office in Sion.

Her morning's handiwork – a network of string and sticky notes – fluttered faintly under the ceiling fan, their corners twitching like restless thoughts. She didn't switch the fan off; she let them flutter, mirroring her own thoughts: unanchored, twitching at the edges.

Restless, she walked to the window and leaned her forehead against the cool pane. Through the grill, she saw a single street lamp flickering – half-tired, half-holding on.

Under its cone of light, a large rat emerged from behind an overflowing bin, dragging a half-eaten ladi of pav nearly twice its size. It paused, nose twitching, before scurrying off.

Everything finds what it's hungry for. Even when it's half-rotten. Even when it's stolen.

She turned back into the room and dropped into her chair like a marionette with cut strings. It wasn't exhaustion that could be cured by sleep. It was the kind that calcified in the heart and made a home in your jaw.

Her mind drifted back to the time when she first met Twarita, and how her friend had entrenched herself in her life. How much Satyadarshi relied on her – for work, order, companionship and an occasional kick to the rear. It was an unsettling day like today when she first laid eyes on her.

It had been a grey October evening when Twarita first walked into the Colaba Police Station just as her shift was starting. She remembered it vividly, though she wasn't sure why it stayed sharper than other cases. The woman with the blood-speckled temple and mismatched slippers stood with her chin tilted stubbornly upward, eyes meeting hers, even as a purple bruise formed a halo around one.

'I want to file a case against my husband,' the woman had said, voice shredded but sure.

There was nothing unusual, not on paper at least. But something about her, perhaps the defiant way she folded her hands behind her back, or the way she refused to shrink, made Satyadarshi take the report herself, though a junior could have easily handled it.

Later that night, against every rule drilled into her, she checked the FIR statement and sent a message to the number there.

Are you alright?

The reply had come quickly.

I'm working on it. Thank you for ... listening. It helped that you treated me like a human being and not an out-of-control woman.

That single text unravelled a thread between them – one that soon thickened into late-night conversations, furious rants, absurd jokes and midnight poetry. It became friendship. Family. The only kind built on broken glass and stitched trust.

It began as a paper trail. It became sisterhood.

It was her case that brought to light the disparity in the treatment, the abuse of power. A case against the son of an ultra-rich Malabar Hill family made waves. The 'higher-ups' hadn't wanted the noise. There were a few veiled threats, mostly to the victim and her family.

A few promises of promotions if she played along.

She never spoke much about the last few cases she had handled in those last months at the force. Twarita never asked.

Some things didn't need to be said. They were written in the scars you didn't show, and the loyalties you didn't have to earn twice. But never once – *not once* – had she regretted what she did.

Satyadarshi smiled at the memory as she looked at the flickering lights outside.

The city outside wasn't silent – it never was. Horns coughed, train tracks groaned under shuddering trains in the distance and someone on a far-off floor thumped closed a metal door. Even Bombay's quiet came with a staccato background noise.

A soft knock made her look up. Then the glass door creaked open, and Twarita stood at the threshold, a paper bag in one hand and two steaming mugs in the other. Her hair was tied up in a lazy bun, loose curls escaping every which way, and she wore an oversized T-shirt that said, 'Detective Fan(g)girl Club – Est. by Me'. She had designed it herself and gifted one set to Satyadarshi, which read, 'The Detective in the Detective Fan(g)girl Club – Est. by Twarita'. She had saved it in her wardrobe, hung in a plastic cover, to keep it safe, much to Twarita's annoyance.

'You again,' Satyadarshi groaned, though the corners of her mouth betrayed her with a twitch.

'Yup, me. Your local well-wisher, sugar addict and designated person-who-makes-you-drink-water-when-you-forget.' She walked in and settled herself cross-legged on the floor like she belonged there. 'Also, I come bearing gifts. Almond butter biscuits. No raisins. Because I care about your psychotic vendetta against raisins – or as you call them, dried grapes.'

'I'd rather eat fresh grapes than those desiccated insults,' Satyadarshi said, her expression turning serious. 'Twa, I'm sorry I dragged you here. Especially at this hour.'

'You didn't drag me, SD. I volunteered. I was watching

Indian Idol Season Who-Cares-They-Are-All-The-Same. You saved me from myself. That's what happens when you love someone – you show up. No matter the time. Or the programme you miss for them.'

The silence that followed was companionable, but fragile – like porcelain held between fingertips. It wasn't awkward. It was old. Familiar between old friends.

Satyadarshi quietly said. 'I think ... Appa might be involved.'

Twarita didn't gasp or flinch as she sat next to her friend. She simply extended a mug of coffee, her eyes saying, go on.

'I found a list of books among Ajoba's papers. Poisons. Misdirection. Oh, and a hidden Nokia phone I examined. Also, a half-torn letter that trails off right before it says something concrete. And that Ajoba knew Laxmi Pancham. I also found the wall hangings present everywhere except Ms Madhyama's emptied bungalow. A library receipt in Appa's name. The fine was for a few books, one on undetectable substances I mentioned above. And it's not just random. Each clue loops back to him – or to Appa. I can't tell where one ends and the other begins.'

She looked up, her eyes vacant. 'This is Appa we're talking about, Twa. The man who cried when I won a bronze medal in a municipal school race. The man who mailed me Carnatic vinyls wrapped in three layers of bubble wrap every year. Who taught me to parallel park using toy cars on the kitchen counter ... '

Twarita's voice, when it came, was soft but sharp. 'Those

memories are genuine, SD. But memory isn't immunity against crime. It doesn't define a person, just what our bodies remember them for.'

Satyadarshi blinked. 'What do you mean?'

'It means even people you love can do things you can't imagine. It doesn't mean they never loved you. It just means you never saw the rest of them, the rest of their personality.'

The coffee scalded Satyadarshi's tongue, and she grimaced. 'What if I'm wrong?' She looked at the organized murder board. 'What if I'm finding connections that don't exist? And if I ask him, and I am wrong, what then?'

'Then you apologize. Bake an eggless vanilla guilt cake for him and write a ten-page sorry letter.' Twarita paused. 'But if you're right, and you turn away ... if you smother your instinct because it doesn't fit your idea of him ... '

She let the sentence hang. Then, in a lower voice, she added. 'I ignored mine once too.'

Satyadarshi's brows furrowed. 'You mean about Ritesh?'

Twarita nodded. 'My own husband called my laugh "embarrassing" in public and made me watch YouTube videos on "laughing in social situations". The entire ... our entire marriage was so confusing, SD. He never hit me. Not really. Not until he did.'

Fidgeting with the coffee mug, she added. 'I knew, rather, my heart knew. Not from my bruises or his yelling. From how my body tensed when he walked into a room. From how I couldn't eat unless he was in a good mood. Or enjoy anything, unless he vocalized his enjoyment. My instincts screamed, but I labelled them dramatic. Overthinking. Because women like me – loud, smart, self-sufficient – don't *get* abused, right? We don't fit the "textbook victim profile".'

Her voice didn't break. It was knotted with old pain that had already bled and scarred. Satyadarshi had heard Twarita's story when she had filed the report, but she had never known the weight of its emotional burden. Her friend had tucked those memories away, and she rarely spoke about them.

'I stayed until the first hit. Then three more. Then I ran. And I promised myself, I would never dull that inner voice again. Never call survival instincts "paranoia".'

Satyadarshi's pulse thudded in her ears. Twarita appeared vulnerable but with a sheen of steel. 'You know, I saw your face the day you came to the police station, the photographs, too. But you always appeared so composed, so in control. Joking, even laughing. Not scared or broken.'

'I didn't let myself break. I couldn't – I was all that was left for myself. And the laughing person you mention? That *is* who I am,' Twarita said. 'But I'm also the girl who spent three months tailing her husband after filing for divorce.'

'You followed him?'

'Of course I did. Once a nerd, always a nerd. It wasn't for the case, I wanted to understand how my judgement could be so flawed.'

'What did you find?'

'Ritesh had two phones. I tracked the other one. That was almost the smoking gun. I found out he had been frequenting a sketchy clinic under a fake name for therapy sessions.

Turned out he had a history of anger issues. Ex-girlfriends, office staff, domestic helpers – all of them were paid off by his father. I had already seen him without his public mask, but I had to *know*.' A half-smile touched her lips. 'That's how I work. Facts. Patterns.'

Satyadarshi stared at her. 'You would make a good PI, Twa.'

'Too bad I already work for an excellent one.'

They laughed – first dry, then loud, a release. It was the laugh that cracked something open. And sealed others.

'Okay, enough of my story. We need to get back to the case. Tell me everything you have found so far,' Twarita said, rising to get her laptop. 'I want to hear it from you again.'

So, Satyadarshi pulled her laptop closer, turned the board towards her, and began.

'The wall hangings ... the animal icons ... the Garuda Mantra. Jai told me about Vault B in the Vishnu temple. Almost all victims had a unique creature with the corresponding colours but the same eagle. And the musical signs. Even the Ragamala drawings, Twa – each was for a different raga. I got confused with the group of ragas mentioned, so I didn't connect the right one to the illustration. But the strange part is, it leads back to Ajoba.'

Twarita listened, nodded and took notes. 'And you think he is Mr Raag?'

'It was an old account, back when phone companies didn't make stringent checks. I don't know. Do you think,' Satyadarshi whispered, 'Ajoba was killed too? That the cancer *caused* his death was just ... camouflage for murder? But the hospital said it was his heart that gave up.' She closed her eyes. 'There's more. Ajoba was "Ni". The seventh swar. The last thread in the pattern.'

Her voice didn't break, but her breath hitched and her eyes shimmered, threatening to water. A single blink might've broken the dam.

Twarita reached out without a word. Her hug was quiet, anchor-like. 'I don't know, SD,' she said, her cheek against Satyadarshi's shoulder. 'But we'll find out. Together. Once we get clarity, *then* we'll grieve. Come on, you were a police officer. Wear your inspector hat again. We need to treat this like any other case.'

Satyadarshi raised her tear-stained face and rubbed her eyes with the back of her hand. 'I'm sure he is somehow involved in this case. But Appa? He complicates things even more. The evidence of books. That *damn* black Titan watch he wears. What if he ... '

'Wait, don't go there. Let's list down everything we know in an Excel,' Twarita said, throwing a baleful look at the board. 'Or wait, let's do it in a notebook. The old-school sleuthing. You said yourself – pen and paper kick-start the brain. Let's go full Poirot.'

They worked for an hour. By the time the sky outside turned indigo, Twarita had created two clean columns: Facts and Feelings. The word 'Appa' appeared in both.

'I want to believe in his innocence,' Satyadarshi said finally. 'But I also want the truth. Even if it breaks me.'

'Then that's what we look for,' Twarita said, squeezing her hand. 'Not a version of the truth. Just the plain, ugly, brilliant and freeing thing.'

In that moment, under a string of yellow tube lights and the buzzing fan, a sense of purpose clicked back into place in Satyadarshi.

Her sleuthing fang gleamed again, finally back on duty.

And Twarita, with a pen behind one ear and her heart on her sleeve, was right where she belonged – beside her.

'We will get to the bottom of this case, Twa. *Then* I will think of Ajoba.'

'Even if the bottom of this case has Appa at it?'

'Even then.'

23

Satyadarshi reached home late on Saturday night to a quiet house. She crawled into bed and hoped sleep would come. When she woke the next morning, she was surprised to find herself well rested. She got dressed with minimal noise – Aai was still asleep – and she wanted to escape before she rose. She pinned a note onto the fridge and, gathering her bag, closed the door behind her.

When she got into a kaali-peeli to the station, her mind buzzed and raced with ideas as the taxi crawled like an injured sloth despite the early hour. People were already out – walking, jogging, doing whatever non-worried people did on Sundays.

She was headed to Appa's house. After their separation, he had shifted to Mulund, and when Satyadarshi messaged him last night, he said he was home and invited her for breakfast.

She reviewed her approach – *confronting would be too harsh. Better to gently broach the topic with Appa.* She knew Vault B was at the centre of this case. Each murder was to gain knowledge of a raga that would be the stepping stone towards opening the door.

What if I started with the book? No, too obvious. The watch? Too confrontational. Maybe I should just … ask if he believes in secrets. No. I can't interrogate him like a suspect. This is Appa.

But … what if he wasn't innocent?

She needed to test her instincts against the facts. Emotion would only cloud her judgement.

Satyadarshi suspected the murders had happened in the order of Sa Re Ga Ma, but she didn't remember the exact dates when each death or attack was first noticed.

The order would decide how the ragas were to be sung. Or maybe the killer followed a haphazard method, because Mr Dhaivat was killed after Ms Pancham. What a tangled case.

She messaged Twarita requesting the details, cursing herself for not carrying the notebook they had filled in last night. Playing with her repaired bag's strap, she checked and rechecked if she had everything inside.

Appa had two tumblers of coffee ready when she rang the doorbell. One look at his open, familiar face had Satyadarshi doubting herself. All the plans, the sequences, the sentences fled her mind when Appa embraced her and asked –

'What was the hurry in meeting me, Kanna? Though I'm not complaining that my only child is here with me.'

I can't do this. No, I need to do this. I can't …

Her gaze wandered around her father's apartment. It was a one-BHK, and he had filled the narrow gap between the window and the metal grille with plants. Mint, tulsi, kadi patta and neem grew in abundance, their greenery creating a pleasant contrast against the shabby walls. *The Hindu*, neatly folded, lay on the futon, waiting to be read.

Appa had decorated his space with minimal fuss. Two futons faced each other, adjacent to the television placed on a table. A few piles of books acted as ad hoc tables, while others leaned against the walls and crowded the passages. On the wall, Appa had hung many pictures – mainly of her, garlanded photos of his parents, Ajoba and Ajji, and a few of Ragini and him in happier times.

He returned from the hole-in-the-wall kitchen – pristine, as expected – with rice murukku arranged on a plate.

They leaned back against the same futon, its cushions strewn about. Satyadarshi reflexively checked if the colour pattern was rainbow. No. It was dull, faded brown. *The rainbow scheme is reserved for members of the septet.*

'How did you know about my Dombivli trip?' she asked, picking up a fried snack and jumping straight in.

'Your Aai told me when I tried calling you but couldn't get through. Why – is there a problem with me knowing it?'

'Appa, this case has bothered me a lot. And it has revealed so much,' she said haltingly.

'I always knew my Satya would crack it. I never doubted your abilities, Kanna. You were always a busybody from childhood. Much like Amma; but don't tell your Aai.'

'Appa, you can drop the pretence. I know everything.' She placed the half-eaten murukku back.

'Drop what? Satya, what are you talking about?' Appa's brow furrowed.

Satyadarshi reached into her bag and brandished the library card. 'This! This card. The Sa Re Ga Ma Pa Dha Ni club. The ragas. The murders. Appa, I know everything. What Ajoba really thought about you. I read his letter. And by the way, I didn't find any box he allegedly left for you.'

'Hey! You found my library card? It's been missing for over six months. Where was it? One day I had it, and the next – gone. I had to beg the librarian, Mrs Kamla, each time.' He reached out for it, but she held it away.

'Drop the act. It's not cutting ice!'

Appa's eyes darted from her hand to her face, trying to locate the joke in her voice. His lips parted, then pressed together. He leaned forward slightly, like a man squinting through the Bombay smog.

'Satya ... have you eaten something strange? What is happening? I don't understand. This is me – Appa. I'm always losing my library card. Everybody knows that!'

'No! You used the knowledge about Ashoka's Unknown Seven – I don't know how, maybe from some history texts – and then you ... harmed those innocent old people into revealing the clues. Ajoba knew it was you. He warned Laxmi about you. He was going to warn Aai as well.'

She knew she was making that last part up. But it was all police training – to trip a person during interrogation.

Appa slumped onto the futon, like a tyre punctured beyond repair. 'You know about Baba's suspicions? How?'

'I found his papers. Why, Appa? Why would you do it?'

'What? What do you think I did?' Realization pinched his

features. 'You think I was behind the killings? No! No! Baba confided a part of his story to me. He and I were very close. Ever since Dhrupad introduced me to him, I became his disciple. What knowledge that man possessed! A great man.'

'Don't lie, Appa!'

'Why should I lie? I loved Baba. Especially since my own father died when I was very young. He was like a father to me – my father by marriage, if not by blood. In me, he saw someone with a fire to learn. He supported Ragini and me when your grandmother protested against our marriage. Why do you think I took up history as a subject, even though mathematics was my first love? To honour Baba.'

Satyadarshi steeled herself. 'Appa, all this emotional drama is fine, but why did you kill Laxmi Pancham?'

'I did not kill her! Baba was worried that someone had discovered his secret group. He was trying to trace who it was. I was helping him in every way possible. Countless meetings. Late-night calls. He didn't tell me the full story, but he didn't have to. He asked for help, and I'd have crossed oceans for him.'

'Yet you left his daughter. Such devotion you display,' she scoffed.

'Satyadarshi! Stay within the confines of respect.'

She pulled out her phone. Her thumb hovered. 'Alright then,' she said, her voice colder than intended, fire burning in her eyes. 'Let's go over your timeline. Where were you on the day Laxmi died?'

'Let me prove it to you! I'll open my schedule. We can clear this up once and for all.'

As she read out the dates of Laxmi Pancham's, Suhel Dhaivat's and Mr Teerth Rishabh Chopra's deaths – courtesy of Twarita – it became clear that Appa had been otherwise engaged.

Laxmi? An all-day conference in Vasai, where he was master of ceremonies. Suhel? A college lecture, complete with a time-stamped video, which he showed her after logging into the college employees' website. Chopra? In Lonavala for a wedding, his voice was audible in a Facebook video where he blessed the bride and butchered a bhajan, with thousands of people laughing. Similarly, for the other killings, he had an alibi, or a near-alibi.

The murders were connected. The probability of them sharing a killer? High.

'You could have hired someone. Or had … an accomplice,' she offered weakly, even as Appa's voice played on loop from the video, singing 'Vaishnav Jan To Tene Kahiye' terribly – he had no ear for music.

He stopped the auto-play and placed his hand over her trembling ones. 'And who would that be, my dearest Kanna?'

Her hazel eyes met his – guilt and anguish storming within – while his brown ones radiated calm. And something worse: forgiveness.

Tears fell unchecked. Appa pulled out a clean white handkerchief from his trousers and gently wiped her face.

She collapsed onto his chest. His arms welcomed her into an embrace.

She wanted to dissolve into the floor. She wanted the pav-dragging rat from last night to come back and eat the part of her brain that made her doubt him. Eat her completely.

What kind of daughter suspects her father of murder? The kind like me ... What had Twarita said? Trust your instincts.

'It's okay. Let it go,' he whispered, rubbing her back as she wept.

She cried because her heart had always believed in Appa's innocence. But she'd let her training override it. The shame of it burned. She felt crushed by her own betrayal, and Appa's magnanimity made it worse.

How can he still love me? How can I ever meet his eyes again?

When the tears stopped, Appa kissed her forehead. 'Satya, I'm at my wits' end. Should I feel offended that my own daughter thinks I'm a serial killer? Or proud that I've raised a bold daughter who questions everything – including me?'

When she didn't respond, he continued, gentler, 'You know what? I'll go with both. You probably think you're worse than sewage. That's the very thing you hate most – the kind that flows through Bombay's gutters. But, Kanna, you did what you were trained to do. You connected the dots, added two and two and got *some* kind of four. Your questions brought you here. Maybe not to the answer we wanted – but to the truth. And that's what matters.'

He gently tilted her chin until she looked at him. 'Tell

me how I can help you. I'll share everything Baba told me. Maybe it'll help.'

She nodded. He patted her head and rose. 'I'll make fresh coffee. It's a long story.'

⁂

She remained seated, fingers tracing the rim of the now-cold tumbler. The cushions still held the imprint of her curled form. On the wall, a photo of her at six – gummy smile, missing front teeth, two plaits ribboned in red – stared back at her as if it knew something she didn't.

From the kitchen came the clang of a steel dabba, the gurgle of milk poured into glasses, and Appa humming 'Karpur Gauram Karunavtaram' under his breath.

How many times had she heard that exact soundscape? When she'd woken early for school and he'd be prepping filter coffee, with *The Hindu* spread open. Aai always swore by the *Times of India*. That was a time when the world made sense – before the murders, before Ajoba's legacy turned into a labyrinth.

Appa returned with a tray carrying two fresh tumblers and a dented biscuit tin. He spread yesterday's newspaper on the floor between them and placed the tray like an offering.

'Baba gave this to me years ago. Told me to keep it safe. I thought it had a will or some boring legal documents. Turns out it had notes.'

She raised an eyebrow. 'Notes?'

He nodded, his gaze far away. 'About music. And faith. And fear. Mostly his.'

'Like?'

'What Baba feared ... it's already begun.'

Satyadarshi stepped out into the diffused sunlight, her thoughts still fogged with the scent of coffee and memory, the biscuit tin tucked under her arm like a relic she didn't know how to hold. She was climbing the station bridge when a shrill announcement stopped her mid-step.

'Attention passengers. Due to Sunday mega block on the Central and Harbour lines, local train services will be delayed or suspended until 2:00 p.m. We regret the inconvenience ... '

Of course. Anyway, it is just a few hours ... can go back to Appa's place, but I don't want to face him yet.

The universe, as usual, had its own sense of timing. She sighed and turned on her heel. No point in waiting at a deserted platform with a broken heart and a half-solved murder chart.

It wasn't just her life that was derailed today.

Resigned, she turned away from the station and wandered down the lane, letting the city's slower weekend rhythm pull her along. Shops were just beginning to open, pulling up dusty shutters; the vegetable vendor on the corner was arguing about methi prices with a lady in a nightie.

Without thinking much about it, she drifted towards the

Johnson & Johnson Garden. It was an old haunt from school excursions, though she hadn't visited it in years. She had always loved its green lawn.

She was sad to see that the garden had aged. The cement benches bore spider-webbed cracks, spreading in all directions. The peepul trees loomed heavier, their roots bulging above the tiled path like veins. Four old men sat in conspiratorial silence, slapping down cards on a stone table with exaggerated grunts. One was smoking a beedi. They eyed her curiously but went back to their game. In a far corner, two boys in oversized cricket pads were squabbling, perhaps over who got to bat next.

Satyadarshi dropped onto a chipped bench under a gulmohar tree, its dry red flowers carpeting the ground like dried blood.

Her hands toyed with the biscuit tin. Her mind didn't want to open it. Not yet.

From somewhere behind the water tank, a boy tried to coax broken notes from a plastic flute. The melody wobbled, off-key and stubborn, but it floated through the late morning like a limp prayer.

She closed her eyes and let it wash over her.

Music was memory, Ajoba had once said. Not notes. Not timing. Memory.

Right now, everything inside her felt slightly out of tune.

Her phone buzzed in her pocket.

Aai. Again.

She stared at the screen until it went dark.

Another gust of dusty breeze rattled the gulmohar branches overhead. She remained seated, letting the sun heat the top of her head, allowing her guilt to bake and fester into something more manageable.

By the time the trains creaked back to life, she had finished her second cutting chai from the tapri outside the garden. The humidity was at its peak, and there was a hint of rain in the air.

And by the time she finally made it home, the shouting had already begun.

24

On the return journey, the train was empty, just like Satyadarshi's mind. She felt depleted – scraped clean of thought, running on fumes and far from solving the case. She had updated Twarita and messaged Jai. He wanted to meet in the evening, but she didn't want to face anyone today.

All the cards are on the table, except one – the one with the killer's name. But it is hidden among the others. Who could it be? Someone who has the knowledge and the wherewithal to commit murder? Appa's clues, helpful, as they were, didn't really change anything.

The whiplashing wind held its silence against Satyadarshi's unending questions. She was exhausted and her swollen eyes were burning. Even though it was only afternoon, she felt her emotions were on a rollercoaster ride from hell.

Pleased as punch. Punched in the gut. Overwhelmed with lust … with a hint of like. Eureka moments. Doggy love. Exhilaration. Dread. Dejection. Guilt. What did I miss? Ah, the taste of the humble pie lingers.

Her stomach rumbled, but she raised a tired hand at her friend, the Goli Vada Pav shopkeeper, too tired to talk to him as her feet slowly dragged her towards the taxi stand. All she wanted to do was curl up in her bed and sleep.

'Bhaiya, Hindu Colony?'

I'm going to tell Aai that I've got a migraine attack. The only way she'll let me sleep in peace.

Their flat hummed when she quietly unlocked the door. Usually, Aai was lounging in her favourite chair, reading, but today the chair stood empty.

Good for me. Fewer questions to answer.

Satyadarshi was heading to her bedroom when she heard voices in Aai's music space. She cocked a weary head and realized it was Aai and Dhrupad Mama fighting.

Again.

She decided to leave them to their devices, thinking that Mama being here would distract Aai long enough for her to wash, change and get into her comfortable, inviting bed.

Satyadarshi tiptoed across the open room and glanced in to figure out where the duelling siblings stood. She had made it across the doorway when something in her uncle's voice stopped her short.

The hair on her neck rose in unison, and she stood next to the door and peeked inside.

The duo stood near the window with the thick curtains tightly drawn, facing each other on opposite sides of Ajoba's desk. Their expressions were stormy, just like the black clouds outside, and they gesticulated to each other wildly.

'No! I have come too far. For years, I saw our father act like a supercilious fool, always turning his nose down at me. I snooped around his office, hoping to find something interesting, but chanced upon something even better! The wretched man held the identity of all the six people, and he practically led me to their door, even though the old crony held the final piece; but he didn't reveal the raga belonging to his team,' Mama spoke in a calm, measured voice, despite his angry expression. His voice held a hint of madness – a controlled, simmering madness.

'Did you harm Baba, Paddu?' screeched Ragini.

Did Aai know about Ajoba's possible murder?

And if she did, why hadn't she told her? A slick, icy hand closed around Satyadarshi's stomach. Ajoba. Her anchor, her hero. Killed. By his own family. The idea slithered inside her, cold and poisonous.

Mama's eyes shone with a peculiar light Satyadarshi recognized as greed. Dhrupad appeared distracted with his story while Ragini stood her ground. Satyadarshi quickly messaged her sole friendly contact at the police, Prateek, with an SOS message and slipped her phone into her pocket. With soft movements, she shrugged her backpack off and placed it against the wall.

Her cell phone vibrated again with a message from Niren Shadaj.

Papa has woken up from his coma. He said he would like to talk to you.

She made a mental note to respond to him later. Dhrupad and Ragini had not noticed her presence. She inched towards the door – a millimetre at a time.

Dhrupad behaved as if he hadn't heard Ragini's question, so lost he was in his rage.

'I should have been the head after Baba. I begged Aai, but she made him promise it would not be me. She said by choosing her husband, she had already gone against the grain and felt it was not the correct choice.'

Spittle speckled Ragini's face, and she flinched, but Dhrupad continued. 'I harangued Baba. But did he listen to me? No! I introduced that Madrasi boy, Raghuram, to him, and that man had the temerity to steal *my* place in our father's life. Suddenly, all Baba could talk about was Raghuram this and Raghuram that! He even got you hooked on the man, fighting with Ajji over the alliance. He was a fool, but what did you see in him?'

Stop, Mama. Just stop. You have no idea what love even looks like, Satyadarshi wanted to say.

Before his sister could respond, he spoke. 'Raghuram has no sense of dressing, no sense of how to behave. Always strutting around in his blue shirts and showing off his clean hankies. Did he ever head an ASI project? No. Do you know why? He didn't have it in *him* to bother. Always licking Baba's heels – he was his dog. Baba's pet dog.'

Wow. I didn't see that coming, and I call myself a detective. Dhrupad Mama is a brilliant actor. To hold such vitriol in his heart and never let even a drop trickle out.

'Paddu! Stop it! You are talking about my husband and my daughter's father,' Ragini shrilled.

'Why? The truth hurts, doesn't it? Like our family hurt me, I want to hurt you!' His arms twitched at his sides, fingers curling into fists.

'You are deranged. Is this why you left the ASI? Snap out of this nonsense immediately,' ordered Ragini.

'Shut up! Don't forget, I'm your elder brother.'

'Then act like one! Why did you quit ASI?'

'ASI? No. I would never leave. The government threw me out. Me! Who was instrumental in discovering the vaults and cataloguing them! They said my effectiveness had run its course. Ha. Who's laughing now? When I open those doors, they will all come crawling towards me. To me. Dhrupad Nishad Phadke.' His voice cracked at his name, and an unhinged sound fluttered free from the cracks.

'Paddu, what are you talking about?' Ragini said, a spark of fear making her voice shaky.

'Baba was going to choose me! Not you, Ragini. Me! It was all decided – Ni for me, Pa for Hariesh. I was *meant* to take over! Until he spat that word "noble" like acid in my face. What did he know?'

He actually spat the word out. 'Noble! Hah! As if he were noble, singing in women's octaves, thinking he was royalty. I was the head of the government's most elite branch that dealt with history and yet I was pushed to the peripheries. I watched, swallowing my hatred, when he told me he chose you. You! You are nothing. Just a failed singer who never developed the courage to even try, go solo or cut an album! How disappointed Baba was in you, and yet he chose you.'

'I ... I ... ' Ragini floundered.

'Well, it doesn't matter now, does it? I'm going to do something Baba could never even dream of doing, Ragu. Hah! Do you know your nickname matches that of your husband, Raghu? Just an "H" extra. H for hideous. H for horrible. H for hated.'

The sudden change of topic flummoxed Ragini even further as she retreated, hitting the wall. Nowhere else to go. Satyadarshi looked around the room in search of something she could use as a weapon. The room was full of stringed musical instruments and a harmonium – all meant to produce sounds of peace. No weapons.

'Where was I?' Dhrupad tapped his index finger on his lips. The light caught his black Titan watch.

The black Titan wristwatch. How did I miss it? He wasn't wearing it when he came home last time.

Her stomach dropped. She saw it now – the black band flashing for half a second in the CCTV footage, the familiar gait she had brushed away as exhaustion, denial. She had been standing inches from Suhel's killer. From her Ajoba's possible murderer. From her own blood.

'Ah, yes. Now, Ragu, be a good girl that you are *not,* and tell me the last raga that Baba entrusted you with. Once I learn that, I will be on my way.'

You won't! Not on my watch.

'What do you intend to do with it?' Ragini asked. Satyadarshi was proud of Aai holding on.

'Intend to do with it? What else, you silly cow? I'm going to sing the Garuda Mantra in the order of the ragas – Bilawal, Khamaj, Asawari, Bhairavi, Marva and the others.'

'Why?'

'Why?! Gosh, you're even stupider than you look. To open the door of Vault B in the Vishnu temple in Kerala.' Dhrupad spoke softly, enunciating each word as if talking to a child.

What do I use to stop Mama from hurting Aai? Think, Satyadarshi, think.

'To get the treasures? They don't belong to you. They're the royal family's property.'

Dhrupad placed his hands on his stomach and laughed. 'Has that ever bothered me? Not taking what isn't mine, Ragu?' He raised his eyebrows. 'Now, enough talking. I want to know the last raga. Right now would be good, wouldn't it, sister of mine?' He stepped closer to Ragini, who cowered, trapped against the wall.

She saw Dhrupad push Ragini, his fists raised high to punch her, and her mother trying to push him away. Satyadarshi picked up the brass cymbals closest to her, reached out and flicked the light switch off, plunging the room into darkness.

'Aai, duck!' she screamed as she flung the cymbals into the dark, praying they hit something vital.

There was a sickening thud of metal clanging, and a grunt of pain answered her.

She flicked the light back on – and saw it: an ugly gash blooming across Dhrupad's temple, blood dripping down his forehead like crimson threads. But it didn't seem to have stopped the man and only made him angrier. He charged at Satyadarshi, murder gleaming alongside the blood in his eyes, screaming in fury.

'You wretched wisp of a girl. Do you think you can stop me? You are like a fly that buzzes around. I'll swat you with one hand. Always following me around. Thwarting my plans!'

He lunged at her, wrapping his meaty hands around Satyadarshi's neck, tightening his grip before she could react. His thumbs pressed down on her throat. His lower body pinned her thighs, stopping her kicks. She pushed at his chest, summoned everything she had, but rage and strength were on Dhrupad's side. Black and white spots exploded behind her eyes; her face burned; she couldn't even gasp.

She struggled, her mind flashing absurd images – Ajoba's wrinkled hands, Aai's crooked lullabies, the cleft on Jai's chin, Baby Bimbette's ridiculous nose, Twarita's jangling earrings, Aai and Appa laughing – everything slipping away.

With the last vestige of strength, she tugged at his wrists, but her hands flailed uselessly as the world tilted.

Blackness rushed in – oily, greedy, like a beast with arms wide open. The next thing she saw – her eyes half-open – was her mother, her dainty five-foot-nothing mother, picking up a four-kilogram tanpura as if it weighed nothing and bringing it down with all her might on Dhrupad's already bleeding temple.

'You never touch my daughter. You got it, Paddu? You don't involve Satyadarshi in this matter. Or any matter,' each word punctuated by a strike of the tanpura.

'Aai, Aai! Stop. He is unconscious. Mama is unconscious!' Satyadarshi managed to choke out between the coughs that wracked her body as she bent over.

Satyadarshi sank to the floor, gasping and the room spun around her. The air scraped her lungs like sandpaper. Her hands clawed at the floor, needing to feel something solid, something real.

I'm alive. Aai saved me. Dhrupad ... Mama was the killer who orchestrated everything ... He can't hurt anyone anymore ...

It struck her with dizzying force. She was alive. A few seconds more, and she might not have been. A sob tore from her throat – half-laughter, half-hysteria – and her blurred gaze locked onto her mother's.

Ragini stopped. She gently placed the instrument on the floor, where it slithered with a well-deserved twang. It had survived to sing its swansong another day. 'Are you okay, Darshi?'

The door crashed open. Uniformed officers flooded the room, weapons drawn.

Satyadarshi instinctively raised a hand, coughing, her voice hoarse. 'It's okay. He's down. There!' she pointed at her uncle.

The police officers hesitated for a heartbeat, surveying the scene – the blood, the tanpura, the battered girl – and then rushed to secure Dhrupad's unconscious body.

Ragini dropped to her knees beside Satyadarshi, her hands fluttering in helpless panic before settling around her daughter's shoulders, anchoring her. 'My baby,' she whispered, rocking her back and forth. 'My brave girl.'

Satyadarshi leaned into her mother, too drained to answer, too grateful to care.

Only when the first handcuff clicked onto Dhrupad's limp wrist did Ragini pull back, her face streaked with tears and determination.

Then she caught sight of the tanpura lying half-twisted on the floor.

She gasped. 'Baba's tanpura!' she cried out, scrambling towards it, checking the strings, the bridge, the hollowed wood with frantic fingers.

'It survived,' she breathed in relief, cradling it to her chest. 'It will sing again.'

Satyadarshi, half-delirious with exhaustion and love, let out a raspy laugh.

Maybe they all would.

The mother–daughter duo watched as the police carried her uncle out, while Prateek stayed back.

Ragini hugged her tighter as they departed, their breaths syncing, the past and present collapsing into the silence between them.

Outside, the sky cracked open with the first thunder of the pre-monsoon.

The storm had finally broken.

And maybe, just maybe, they were ready to begin again – one note at a time, all in the same sur.

Epilogue

Now

'Kanna, let me get you some more coffee. Or would you prefer hot lemon tea?' Appa's French beard tickled her ears as he got up from the chair next to her, picking up her cup from the table.

'Neither, Appa. It's too muggy for anything, and Aai just made a gross cup of turmeric milk for me. She said it would heal my injuries faster. Who can argue with her? I definitely don't have the strength to.'

The father–daughter duo smiled with affection as Ragini bustled into the room, apron strings fluttering behind her. She drew the curtains of the living room, and the room turned a few shades darker and a few degrees cooler.

'What are you guys giggling about? Darshi, don't overuse your throat. You know I'm the expert when it comes to taking care of throats. And I say no more talking. I've made ragi upma with vegetables and oodles of ghee as it's good for your throat. Raghu, you're staying for dinner.'

Satyadarshi sneaked a look at Appa's smiling eyes and obediently nodded. 'Yes, Aai.'

Ragini scooted next to her daughter. Her fingers moved gently over the bruises on Satyadarshi's neck, now turning a stormy shade of purple against her fair skin. Dhrupad's thumbprints, sharp and undeniable, marked her throat with a music only violence could compose. 'I'm so sorry, Darshi. I just can't imagine my brother doing something like this. To his only niece … it's unbelievable!'

'Aai, let it go.' Satyadarshi's voice was roughened but steady. 'Mama wasn't in his right mind. The temple, the ASI sacking … it broke him. These bruises will fade in a week or two. And honestly, it already feels like everything happened a lifetime ago.' Even though swallowing was a lot more painful than she let on.

Appa clattered about in the kitchen, rinsing the cups they had used before returning and wiping his hands. Satyadarshi patted the seat beside her, inviting him into their little cocoon. Wordlessly, he sat. She took her mother's hand in one of hers and leaned her head against Appa's familiar shoulder, the one that had carried her on toddling feet to the very edge of music.

They sat, braided together by silence, bruises and old songs. Yesterday's storm had abated and for a short while, they were a unit of three again.

For the first time in days, she let herself simply breathe. Appa's shoulders were still strong, but she could feel the slight stoop now, the invisible curve of time. She looked at her parents, and a disquieting thought entered, unfettered, into her brain. *When did they get so old?*

'Appa and Aai, I wanted to talk to you and get the complete story out. I think Appa is aware of a few pieces of the jigsaw puzzle, and some are with Aai. Now that we are here together, let's finish solving the puzzle. Right here, right now,' she rasped.

Appa placed a kiss on her temple. 'Where to begin, Satya? Ah, first, let me tell you, your friend, Jai, and might I add, what a handsome and well-mannered chap he is. He was so concerned when he heard about your attack. Immediately, he rushed to the hospital at night, Kanna. And he stayed there too. He is a keeper.'

'And Twarita,' added Ragini, 'terrorized the nurses to make sure you were seen first. You've got a good team.'

Satyadarshi raised her head and rolled her eyes at her father. 'Stop dodging, Appa.' She buried her face in his chest and her smile, too. *It was good to see Jai.* She could hear the echo of her father's chuckle deep inside.

'For once, I agree with your father, Darshi. Jai has such beautiful eyes, and he is so smart! Raghu, do you know he is also a fan of your favourite subject – history!' chimed in Ragini.

The estranged husband and wife shared a knowing look. Their mirth eased the tension. Satyadarshi elbowed Appa to make him get serious, and finally, he launched into the tale.

'Ouch! Where was I? The secret society Ashoka founded didn't end with his reign, Kanna. It grew, adapting across centuries. Every generation handed down a thread of knowledge – the Sa, Re, Ga, Ma, Pa, Dha, Ni. The idea was simple: if a leader had no child or found their firstborn unfit, they could choose a worthy successor.'

His hand brushed Satyadarshi's hair absently, his voice dipping into memory. 'Sa was headed by Mr Shadaj, who wants to retire after the incident, so he has passed the lead to his son, Niren. They were in charge of alchemy.'

Ragini added quietly, 'Most of us didn't know the full web of ties anyway. Even if they sensed a link, the septet always kept their strands separate, and family members were discouraged, sometimes outright forbidden, from talking about it beyond their own notes.

Appa nodded. 'That's why communication is always the key. To continue, Re is now Naad's, and he is already engrossed in microbiology. Ga lies with Geeta, although she is struggling a bit with sociology.'

Satyadarshi listened, spellbound, as the missing notes were filled in. *The next generation kicks in.*

'Shaila has returned from the US, and she is familiarizing herself with Ma – she's studying physiology. Whereas Hariesh inherited Pa from his Nani, warfare. Dha … ' Appa hesitated. 'Dha's seat is vacant. Mr Dhaivat left no clear heir. They'll have to choose someone new.'

'Preferably someone who understands cosmogony,' Ragini said softly.

'The notes shift,' Appa said, 'but the melody carries on. Always.'

'And Ni?' Satyadarshi asked, even though she already knew.

Ragini smiled, weary but luminous. 'Ni was entrusted to me. Communication. Music.'

The word hung in the air between them, thick and golden.

'Appa, in the olden days, I understand there were secrets and treasures that had to be protected, but what would you be doing now? All treasures belong to the state or central government,' whispered Satyadarshi, trying not to strain her voice.

Ragini answered, not Appa. A mischievous smile played peekaboo on her lips. 'Because some treasures aren't measured in gold or land deeds, Darshi. Some secrets are truths that would destroy more than they preserve.'

'You mean ... there might be *more* undiscovered vaults in the Vishnu temple?' Satyadarshi belted out. Ragini just shrugged, so she added. 'Or other places?'

Ragini laughed. 'Your time will come, Darshi. You will be privy to all the answers then.'

'If Hariesh already knew about the septet, why did he hire me? He could have solved the case then and there, Aai!' Satyadarshi squeaked painfully.

'If only he had known, right? You did ask him about music, but grief fogs the mind, and Hariesh was broken. I'm still learning how all these fit together myself. It takes time, and Laxmi died before she could explain everything. By the time he could gather himself, you'd already connected the dots. It took *you* to see the whole tapestry. That's why only you could solve it – as music runs in your blood, Darshi,' Ragini said.

Satyadarshi closed her eyes and leaned against the backrest, letting out a sharp breath. 'So, everyone, even Aai, had an inkling, even then! If we had just talked, the case could have been wrapped up faster.'

'Ho. But I didn't know about Paddu, na? I wasn't aware of how much bitterness he had been nursing – for me, for your Appa. He'd always been a little strange from his childhood, but we were always taught to ignore and forgive the shortcomings of family. That's our Indian way. If we had him tested on time, maybe this would've not gone the way it did. Maybe we forgave too much.'

Satyadarshi nodded, her throat tight.

'Satya, the police recovered your Ajji's missing notebooks in his Goregaon flat. Now Ragini can use those compositions! And I think they discovered several hawan kunds there, didn't they?' Appa asked gently.

She nodded. 'Five. At least. The neighbours in his society said the chanting never stopped – night after night.' Her voice cracked. Ragini placed a hand on her daughter's mouth. 'Darshi, don't speak so much,' she admonished.

'Aai, I'll stop soon. Dhrupad Mama made a ruckus in custody, had to be sedated and finally moved to the psych ward in the prison hospital.' She whooshed out a bubble of air. 'He will probably be declared incompetent to stand trial and would remain there. But who knows?'

'He deserves to be there for trying to harm you. And of course, killing our friends. Paddu not getting the death penalty is the most generous thing that could happen to him.'

Satyadarshi shifted slightly, resting her chin on her palm. 'The watchman at the Panchams' society admitted he'd been passing along details of the staff's comings and goings to Mama for a few hundred rupees. Oh, by the way, we found out something strange about the gun that killed Suhel Dhaivat. The police found it wrapped in a yellow cloth with a tilak on it,' she said, her voice still coming out in staccato beats. 'It's a Glock – almost impossible to get here legally.'

Appa raised his brows. Ragini leaned forward.

'My friend at the police, Prateek, dug around quietly. Turns out the handgun matches a batch of weapons that went missing from a royal family's private collection in Gujarat, back in the late '90s. No official police report. They buried the scandal.'

Her parents exchanged a loaded glance.

'I think Dhrupad Mama somehow ... *acquired* it. Maybe when he was still in the ASI, dealing with royal inventories.' She shrugged, the tiredness pulling at her smile. 'The police will surely add "smuggler" to his list of qualifications.'

Appa muttered something under his breath that sounded suspiciously like 'madman.' Ragini just pressed her daughter's hand, anchoring her back to quieter waters. Then, frowning, Appa raised his voice.

'Ragini, Satya, I still have suspicions about Dhrupad killing Baba. Did he confess it outright?'

'No, Appa. But from everything we know, it's likely he poisoned his own father, our Ajoba, with an undetectable drug. For that act itself, I hope he suffers,' said Satyadarshi, bitterness coating her words.

'I don't know how much more time Baba had with us, Darshi. He may be gone, but he remains in our music; and in this house, in you and in me.' She hesitated, hands fiddling in her lap, then added, almost shyly, 'I'm thinking ... maybe a concert. A small one. Diwali Pahat in Pune.'

Appa and Satyadarshi burst into applause for Ragini's sake, who flushed, laughing like a girl again.

Warmed by the sound, Satyadarshi closed her eyes.

But there was one last puzzle piece gnawing at her.

'Appa, Aai, there's this one question that is very high on my mind,' she said, as she held her parents' hands in hers. 'Why did you guys split up?'

The question floated between them, heavy and gentle all at once.

Ragini and Raghuram exchanged a long look. One full of years, fights, songs, regrets.

'Oh, I forgot to tell you, Darshi, Twarita had called. I told her you were resting. She said a new client had mailed her about a case that he wanted you to handle,' deflected Ragini, giving a pointed look at the marks covering Satyadarshi's neck. 'You decide what you want to do. You know how I let you make your own decisions.'

Satyadarshi's eyes flashed at Appa, and they exchanged a knowing smile.

'I'll decide tomorrow,' she murmured, reaching for a rainbow cushion to snuggle into, and closed her eyes, sinking into the softness of the sofa, the hum of her parents' breathing around her.

Every day was a new sur, after all.

And tomorrow?

Tomorrow was another day.

Then

The tanpura thrummed in Ajoba's hands, its deep, resonant hum filling the tiny living room with music older than memory. The red string flapped in the air.

Little Satyadarshi, no more than six years old, sat cross-legged at his feet, her toy harmonium balanced precariously on her lap. Her stubby fingers pounded wrong notes with the determination of a warrior, each discordant sound followed by a tiny, earnest voice trying to match the melody.

She was singing. A little off-key, a little too loud, but with the fierce sincerity of a child who believed music could fix anything broken, anything sad. Her Ajji had told her that when you want to cry, you should remember your favourite song. The ache will quiet itself.

Ajoba laughed, the sound bubbling out of him, warm and easy, like a river tumbling over familiar stones.

'Darshi, my chakuli, sur is not about singing loudly,' he said, placing the tanpura beside him.

'It's about finding the right note inside you. Not forcing it.'

She made a face, her lower lip jutting out in frustration. 'But Ajoba, if I sing louder, won't it come faster?'

He chuckled. She loved the sound of his laughter, it was a soft rumble that made the brass bells near the window tinkle in response. Bending closer so his forehead nearly touched hers, he whispered, as if entrusting her with a secret.

'Sur isn't a race, Satyadarshi. It's a search. A promise. Sometimes, it takes a lifetime to get it right.'

He tapped her gently on the chest, right above her heart.

'But once you find it here,' he said, 'no one – not even the biggest storm – can take it away from you.'

Outside, the first rumble of the monsoon split the sky, the scent of wet earth curling into the room like a blessing. It made everything feel alive, fresh, like a new beginning.

Inside, Ajoba plucked the tanpura strings again, their vibration shimmering in the thick, expectant air.

Satyadarshi scrunched her nose in fierce concentration, pressed a hesitant key on her harmonium.

Her voice followed a moment later. It was still slightly shaky, still slightly sweet, but this time, it landed true.

Ajoba closed his eyes and smiled. When he looked at his granddaughter, his heart leapt. She would go far, he knew. Farther than any of them.

Especially with a name like hers – Satyadarshi, the one who sees the truth. A truth-seeker, destined to carry the baton of Ni when the time came, and perhaps change the course of things.

But for now, she was just a little girl, and he only wanted to savour her childhood a little longer.

He heard her sing – hesitant, but true – and he knew: the talent was already there.

Outside, the rain began to fall.

Inside, a note had found its home.

And the tanpura remembered.

Acknowledgements

Only genuine book lovers read the acknowledgements. So, to you, dear reader: welcome, and thank you.

Writing a book is its own kind of madness. Finishing it is a miracle. But watching your dog, Biscuit, sniff the manuscript and wag approvingly? That's when you know you're onto something.

My deepest gratitude, as always, goes first to my mother, Harsh Mani, who raised me on stories, letters and the gentle tyranny of good grammar. To my father, Capt. Harish Chander (INS), for teaching me to notice the small, often overlooked details – because plot twists, like naval salutes, depend on precision. And to Col. Arun and Manju Sawarkar, who gave me my earliest compass for right and wrong, books and beliefs. Without Ajay Sawarkar and his quiet, unwavering support, I wouldn't be writing to you today.

To my mentor, Dr Mathew T. J. – your absence echoes on every page.

To Purba, the only person I know capable of launching a literary career by hurling a pen at someone's face. Thank you for guiding me patiently through every music-related rabbit hole. And to Dipali Aunty, in whose music room I first saw a tanpura – it all began there.

To Team Penmancy, Kajal, and Rham, for introducing me to a circle of writers and thinkers who became part of my scaffolding: Alpna, Anamika, Anagha, Amita, Aparna, Chandra, Deepa, Manali, Manoshi, Narayani, Nilshree, Priya, Ranjani G, Shweta, Shweta S, Supriya, Sangeetha Kamath, Parag and many more.

To Aekta, Jayanthi, Sheerin, 'our' Sudha, Sonal, Urmi – thank you for entering my life not like plot devices, but like essential subplots.

Khushboo, Lalitha, Monica, Shalini and Sangeetha: the women who've heard every melodramatic voice note, survived my plot spirals, endless rants and chai-fuelled existential crises, and still message me with love (and memes). I don't know what karmic jackpot I hit, but I hope I never have to return it. #SoulSisters #CertifiedCrisisCrew

To the friends who hover protectively like umbrellas in unpredictable weather: Anithra, Anshul, Dimple, Dwayne, Mehr, Mohita, Pallavi, Pooja, Sailee, Seema, Sheetal, Shubhangi.

A giant shoutout to my St. Xavier's College tribe, especially Raul and Ryan, my go-to venting buddies for everything from gossip cravings to my-life-sucks rants. And to my Fr Agnel's School Girl Gang, you gals rock and are my rock.

Gratitude to Gaurav for introducing me to Mr Ajit Avadhani, whose help was peerless.

Pratima, Sanjay, Sahil, Siya, Raj Bhaiya, Neetu, Tarun, Achintya, Kamlesh and Narendra Nath – you're irreplaceable.

This book wouldn't exist without Shreya Ahlawat, editor extraordinaire, who wields her red pen with a surgeon's finesse and a poet's intuition. And to Pujitha Krishnan, who saw what this story could become, even before I did. A special thank you to Simran Chanana, whose meticulous edits sharpened every line and to Vidisha Ghosh, for catching the gremlins I didn't even know existed. To the Pan Macmillan India team, thank you for the faith and the fire. Meghna Menon – your cover caught the soul of this story before even the blurb did.

My agent, Lalitha Ravindran, thank you for being the calm in my creative storms, and for believing in me. And to the First Forays authors and fellow travellers on this wild journey, cheers to us.

An ocean of gratitude for Himanjali Sankar, Kiran Manral, Meeti Shroff Shah and Vish Dhamija – thank you for your generous support, belief and kindness.

Chaitanya, Naisha and Biscuit – the three beings who shape my days in completely different, equally powerful ways. And yes, Biscuit, thank you for sniffing Satyadarshi and Jai and giving their chemistry your signature tail-thump of approval. You're the only critic I trust (and love) unconditionally.

To every author whose work reminds me to keep going, to every early reader who sent a message of encouragement, to every unnamed hero of the journey – know that this book carries you too.

And to Satyadarshi, who wouldn't stop yakking until I wrote her story. Then came Baby Bimbette, cryptic clues and a murder playlist that hijacked my life. She has plans. Resistance is futile.

If I've missed anyone, please blame the deadline, not the sentiment. This book, like all books, was never written alone.

Thank you for the love. And for those reviews on Amazon and Goodreads.

Love,

Natasha